JO BARNES studied English at Leeds University and for 25 years taught children and young people from ages 3 to 19 in London schools. Then she became a writer.

She had an extensive knowledge of children's books, partly because she enjoyed reading them so much! She knew exactly what children liked because she regularly read to her own as well as those in school.

Odd Fox Out is the first of Jo's books to be published, and will be followed by two more in 2024.

Odd Fox Out

Jo Barnes

SilverWood

Published in 2023 by SilverWood Books

SilverWood Books Ltd
14 Small Street, Bristol, BS1 1DE, United Kingdom
www.silverwoodbooks.co.uk

Fox painted by Reena Patel, inspired by istock/bazilfoto

ISBN 978-1-80042-247-6 (paperback)

British Library Cataloguing in Publication Data
A CIP catalogue record for this book is
available from the British Library

Page design and typesetting by SilverWood Books

For Tony, who stopped eating animals when it was a really weird thing to do.

Contents

CHAPTER ONE

The Rappin' Rabbit

It was a beautiful late afternoon in spring and I couldn't get rid of the beetle in my mouth. I'd been chewing for ages but I couldn't seem to swallow it and it wasn't even easy to spit out. At least it had stopped wriggling, probably because it was in pieces now. And then the legs started to get stuck between my teeth. And it wasn't even as if it tasted nice! No wonder my mum put honey on them. Mm...honey-glazed beetle bites. This one didn't taste like that at all.

But it was *my* beetle that I'd caught myself! My first ever catch! Who'd have thought that it would change my life.

Forever.

Because that's when I heard sniggering. Someone was laughing at me – almost certainly my sister Ethel. I'd been so proud of myself, catching a beetle, and now she was laughing at me! Typical. She always had to spoil things. But when I turned my head, feeling ready for a fight, I saw...not Ethel, but a tiny grey-brown bundle of fur with long ears, a twitchy nose and a vaguely familiar scent.

"That looks yuck," it said. "Why don't you chew some grass

to get the taste out of your mouth?"

I just stared at it.

"Oh, all right then, ignore me," it said. "I was only trying to be helpful."

"You're a..." I said. "But you can talk!"

"Course I can!" it snorted. "Did you think I was a baby?"

My mouth started to water. Something told me I wasn't acting the way a fox was supposed to act.

"Excuse me," I said at last. "You *are* a rabbit, aren't you?"

The rabbit hit its head with one of its front paws.

"Duh! Oh, well done. And what's this big thing here? Could it be – let's see now – a tree?"

Oh, being clever now, was it?

"Well, I've never talked to a rabbit before! I didn't even know rabbits *could* talk."

The rabbit's mouth dropped open.

"Duh!" it said again. "How could we do anything if we couldn't talk? How could we dig, like, great big warrens with lots of cosy homes inside, if we couldn't talk?"

"Dunno," I said. "Hadn't thought about it. I've only ever talked to foxes. You rabbits keep out of our way."

The rabbit nodded.

"We have to, you know." It lowered its voice as if it was telling me a secret. "There are lots of dangerous creatures out to get us rabbits."

Then it looked at me, and put a paw to its mouth. I heard it muttering something.

"Owl or hawk...weasel or stoat...fox or..."

It stopped.

"What's the matter?" I said.

The rabbit didn't move. Its eyes were staring and it started to shake.

"Are you all right?"

I came closer. All its cockiness had vanished. It was frozen with fear.

My heart started to thump. I glanced around. Could the rabbit see something? Something behind me? It was getting darker. Perhaps I should just scoot off home.

"What...what are you afraid of?"

The rabbit's eyes flickered.

"You," it whispered.

"What?" What was it talking about? "*I'm* not gonna hurt you! You weren't worried just now – what happened?"

"I forgot the rap."

"The what?"

"The dangerous creatures rap."

And a flame suddenly sparked to life in my brain. Of course! That's what I'd been doing wrong. You weren't supposed to *talk* to rabbits. You were supposed to *eat* them! Roast rabbit, with me and my sisters fighting over who had the hind legs. Rabbit stew, its mouth-watering smell wafting round the earth at supper time.

The rabbit started to shiver violently and sob, "I want my mum."

What?

This wasn't supposed to happen! Surely rabbits didn't *mind* being eaten. That was what they were for, after all. They weren't supposed to go round crying for their mums.

"It's all right, it's all right," I said. "Don't cry. I'm not gonna hurt you."

"Oh yeah?" it sniffled. Slowly, slowly it started to back away.

"I'm not, honest. Look… I know… I know I'm supposed to kill you…but I… I dunno… I can't."

The sniffs grew quieter.

"Honest?"

"Honest. Like I said – I've never talked to a rabbit before, and, well, now that I've met you… I can't *eat* you."

"Never mind *you*," gulped the rabbit. "My *mum*'ll kill me if she finds me here. She made me say that rap hundreds of times, and then I go and forget it."

"What *is* this rap thing?"

The rabbit wiped its paw across its nose.

"You sure you're not gonna hurt me?"

"Yeah, honest."

"Promise?"

"Oh, get on with it!"

"All right, well, see, it used to be this boring poem." Sniff. "And then this group of young rabbits got together and called themselves 'The Rappin' Rabbits'." Sniff. "They're awesome!" it said, its eyes shining. "They talk like this, 'Yo, be cool, bro.'" It started to giggle again, then it looked at me and shuffled a bit further away. "Anyway, they turned this poem into a rap, and this is how it goes now."

It sat up and started to thump one of its hind paws on the ground. Then after another sniff, and swaying in time to the beat, it waved its front paws to and fro. The beat was catchy and by the time the rabbit started to chant I was swaying along with it.

"Close to home or wand'rin' far,
Remember this song wherever you are:
Owl or hawk,
Don't stop to talk, bro.

Weasel or stoat,
They'll be at your throat, bro.
Fox or crow,
You'd better just go-go.
Dog or man,
Escape if you can, yo.
A-*one* and a-*two* and a-three four *five*,
This is the rap that'll keep you ALIVE."

The rabbit finished with a flourish, both front paws up in the air. Then it sat and looked at me as if it expected me to say something.

"Er – that's very good," I said, "but...what's a dog? I know what a dog-fox is, but what's a dog?"

"I don't know!" wailed the rabbit. "So I'll probably get eaten by one."

It crouched on the ground and started sobbing again.

"Look," I muttered. "Just go home, will you. And don't talk to anyone except other rabbits, if you really want to stay alive."

Still sniffing, it backed off slowly until it was too far away for me to jump on.

Then it sat up and started to look a bit cocky again.

"Why've you got one white paw?" it asked.

"Dunno," I said. "Just born like it."

"I never seen a fox with one white paw," it went on.

"Well, how many foxes *have* you seen? Not many, I reckon. You didn't even realise I *was* a fox at first."

"Course I did! I just forgot I was s'posed to run away!"

And it turned and skipped into the bushes.

I sat down on the cold, damp ground and felt that everything around me had changed. The trees looked the same, with fresh green leaves bursting out on their branches. The spring flowers looked the same, snuggling purple and white in the grass. But somehow…everything had changed. A ripple had passed through the wood. The world had shifted and nothing made sense any more.

So rabbits were clan-folk, who lived in families, like foxes. They talked to each other and had feelings, just like foxes. Then why did other clan-folk eat them? Kind ones, like my mum. What else was I going to find out? Perhaps chickens were clan-folk too. But no, they looked too stupid.

I was still gazing into space when Ethel jumped on me and knocked me over.

"Ha! Gotcha!" She stopped and sniffed around. "Hey, cool – I smell rabbit! Let's track it down!"

I picked myself up.

"No, don't let's!" I said.

Ethel stared at me.

"Why not?"

"Because…because it's late…and Mum will be worried. And besides," I went on, "it must be a really old scent, because I've been here for *ages*, and I haven't seen a *single* rabbit!"

Ethel sniffed again. "It smells quite fresh to me. But it *is* late, and I'm starving."

She turned and trotted in the direction of home and I followed her in a daze. All I could think about was the sobbing rabbit, crying for its mum.

And there was the big beech tree, with our earth underneath. And there was *my* mum, with her head poking out of the entrance.

"Thank goodness, I was beginning to get worried. Hurry up, I've made a lovely rabbit stew for supper."

CHAPTER TWO

Are Wood Mice Clan-folk?

After that, life started to get difficult. I didn't want to eat rabbit, but there didn't seem to be much else *to* eat. Wood mouse rolls used to be one of my favourites, but they didn't taste quite the same any more. Were wood mice clan-folk, like rabbits? I just didn't know. But I fell on a bowl of chicken and bolted it down.

A few days later, it was rabbit stew again. I knew by the smell, even before it was on the table. I was hungry, too. I looked around at my family, sitting in our cosy underground home.

"You're safe underground," Dad always said. "Nothing can touch you here."

Shadows flickered on the rough earth walls. But they were friendly shadows, with pointed ears and noses and Mum's bushy tail waving round as she prepared supper. At one end of the room was the oven, built of stones heaped right up to the smoke-hole in the roof. The fire at the bottom glowed orange and red. Our hungry faces were lit by a fat tallow candle in the middle of the upturned log that was our table. Me, my two sisters and my dad, all waiting for the rabbit stew. What was I going to do?

Home. How snug it was. How mouth-watering the supper smelt. I wanted everything to stay like this forever. I didn't want to cause trouble, to be the odd fox out, to tell my family I thought they were doing something wrong.

Mum carefully lifted an earthenware dish from the piping hot stones inside the oven. The wet leaves around her paws began to steam as she carried it to the table.

"Mm, my favourite," sighed Elfreda.

"You're lucky then – we're always having rabbit," said Ethel. "We haven't had vole pie for ages."

"It takes a lot of voles to make a good-sized pie," explained Mum, spooning stew into our bowls. "It's the same with the mice. You need so many of them."

"What about roast chicken?" I said. "We haven't had that for a while either."

Dad thumped his paw on the table.

"Be thankful for what you've got," he said sternly. "When winter comes, you'll be begging for a bowl of rabbit stew!"

I pushed my bowl away.

"No thanks, I'm not hungry," I said.

"What is it, Edgar?" said Mum. "You don't seem to want to eat anything but chicken. Your father can't keep risking his life going to the farm, you know. There are dogs there, and humans with killing sticks."

"I'm not afraid of any old stick!" shouted Ethel.

"Then you're sillier than I thought," said Dad. "These aren't ordinary sticks. They make a noise like thunder and shoot hard little things at you, like stones, but not made of stone. If one of those hits you you're dead."

But I wasn't interested in killing sticks. There was that word the rabbit had chanted in its rap.

"What's a dog?" I asked.

"A dog, my son," said Dad, "is a creature something like a fox, but he's our greatest enemy. You remember that big black animal we saw when I took you to look at the farm – that was a dog. They can run like us and follow a scent like us. They have sharp teeth like us, but they're often much, much bigger than us – sometimes twice as big or even more. A dog, my son, is deadly."

"So you see," said Mum, "we don't want your father to go risking his life too often just to bring us chicken, do we?"

"No, Mum," I said, and blew on my bowl. Then I slurped up a mouthful. It tasted so good that I managed a few more, but I couldn't get that rabbit out of my head. Had the one I was eating cried for its mum, when Dad had killed it?

Later that evening, curled up with my sisters in our bedroom and drifting half asleep and half awake, I heard Mum and Dad talking.

"You know, Hilda," said Dad, "I think it's time we took these youngsters on a chicken raid."

"Oh, Alfred, they're so little," said Mum. "They haven't even got their proper colour coats yet."

"They've got to learn," said Dad. "Young Edgar seems to think I can magic chicken out of the air."

Mum didn't say anything, but I heard her creep into our bedroom. I opened one eye.

"Are you going to tell us a story?" said Elfreda, opening both eyes.

"Would you like one?" said Mum.

"Yeah!" I said. "Tell us some more about the Spring Hare. I love her."

Elfreda sat up.

"Does she only come in springtime, or whenever anyone's in trouble?" she asked.

"Well, I've never heard of her coming at any other time of year," said Mum, "but I can't be sure."

"If I saw a hare I'd jump on it and eat it!" said Ethel.

"Don't be ridiculous!" said Mum. "As if you could eat the Spring Hare! She's not like an ordinary hare. She's there to help us all."

"I don't believe in her," said Ethel. "I think she's just one of those stories that grown-ups tell cubs to make them feel happy."

"You can believe what you like, Ethel," said Mum. "All I know is that my grandmother saw her once, and it saved her life. Did I tell you about it?"

"Yes, but tell us again," I said. I loved this story!

"Now let's see. It was late in the springtime, almost summer," she began. "The moon was shining brightly – the Hare loves the moonlight, you know – and my grandmother was a carefree young vixen. It was such a lovely warm night that she decided to go hunting all on her own."

"Cool!" said Ethel. "Did she pounce on a juicy bunny and grip it with her teeth and bite it and bite it till the blood spurted all over her and..."

"Be quiet, Ethel! This is not that sort of story!"

Mum glared at Ethel, who just smirked back.

"Now what my grandmother didn't know was that a huntsman had been in the woods that day, setting his traps. Awful cruel things they were, with jagged teeth. If one of them bit into your leg, it'd never let you go.

"One of these traps had been set on the very path my grandmother decided to go down. It was hidden under the leaves, so no one could see it. But just as she was about to step on it she heard her name called softly from behind.

"'Winifred, Winifred,' called this lovely voice. It was like cool water trickling in a little brook on a hot summer's day. That's what my grandmother said.

"'Who's there?' gasped grandmother, but nobody answered. Then out of the trees danced a beautiful Hare, all silvery and shimmering. She brushed aside the leaves and put one of her front paws in the trap. It snapped shut with a horrible crack."

I couldn't help shuddering, though I knew what was going to happen next.

"The Hare just pulled her paw out of that trap as if it were made of old twigs, but it stayed shut, so it couldn't hurt anyone else. Then she smiled at my grandmother and danced away in the moonlight."

A little bubble of happiness travelled along from my tummy and came out of my mouth as a sigh.

"And what would have happened if the Hare hadn't been there?" asked Elfreda.

"My poor grandmother would have been caught in that trap, in great pain, with her leg broken, until the huntsman came along and shot her," said Mum. "So don't go telling me you don't believe in the Spring Hare."

"She could have dreamt it," said Ethel.

Mum shook her head and licked us goodnight.

I looked dozily at my sisters, already snoring softly. Well, *I* believed in the Spring Hare, even if Ethel didn't. But...if only I could see her. Then I'd *know* she was real.

CHAPTER THREE

The Raid

"Don't mind the squawks, don't mind the pecks!
We'll rip their heads from off their necks!
We'll scrunch their bones, then home we'll fly
For Mum to bake a chicken pie!"

We were finally going to the chicken farm. Ethel and Elfreda were doing this mad war dance, chanting faster and faster as they leapt around, and I lay watching them with my nose on my paws.

Suddenly Ethel stopped and cocked her ears towards me.

"Hey, saddo," she panted. "Doesn't ickle Edgar want to go hunting then?"

"Shut up!" I said. "Course I do, but it's not really a hunt, is it? It's more of a raid, 'cos we know where the chickens are to start with. Anyway, yeah, it'll be good – so long as it's only chickens."

"What d'you mean, 'only chickens'?"

"Well, I mean, I don't mind killing chickens, that's all. Like – chickens aren't clan-folk – you know, not like rabbits and things..." I trailed off.

They both gaped at me. Then Ethel guffawed.

"He's gone nuts!"

"What *do* you mean, Edgar?" panted Elfreda, lying down beside me.

"Well... I mean," I stammered. How could I explain? "Well, when Dad took us to look at the farm that time, the chickens were just sort of pecking round stupidly and...well, they didn't look as if they could be clan-folk, with feelings and things like us. Know what I mean? Like...they even need a human to look after them. But...if you think about rabbits building warrens and things, and looking after themselves...well, they must sort of be clan-folk, a bit like us...sort of..."

Elfreda shook her head. "You can't think like that, Edgar. I think rabbits *are* clan-folk, but they're not *our* sort of clan-folk. It's the way of the wild. Foxes have always eaten rabbits, so there can't be anything wrong with it."

Then Mum and Dad appeared.

"Come on, you lot," said Dad, "no messing around."

"And be careful," said Mum. "We don't want anyone getting hurt."

"The wind's blowing in the right direction tonight," said Dad. "But if it changes, we stop and come back. No sense taking any chances where dogs are concerned – or humans who might have killing sticks. Any questions before we start?"

"Yes," said Elfreda. "Are you quite quite sure that the dogs'll be chained up?"

"They always are at night," Dad explained. "They let them loose in the daytime, when the hens are pecking round in the field. I think they must be trained not to touch them. But at night the chickens sleep in a henhouse so they don't need guarding. At least, that's what the humans think, so they chain the dogs up."

"So if they're chained up, why should we be afraid of them?" I asked.

"Because," said Dad, "of the awful racket they make. If they know we're there, they'll bark and bark, and wake up the humans, who'll come and untie them, and perhaps even shoot at us. Understand? Now let's go."

Once we were on the move my worries vanished. It felt as if we were all one creature, not five different foxes, loping silently through the trees. Our night eyes could see everything as if it was daylight and our ears picked up every tiny rustle in the undergrowth. It was great being a fox!

At the edge of Horn Wood, we stopped and looked carefully around. There was one field to cross before we reached the farm.

"What can you smell, children?" whispered Dad.

We lifted our noses.

"Rabbit!" whispered Elfreda. "Quite close, I think, Dad."

"Very good, dear," said Mum, "but we're not bothering with that tonight, Alfred, are we?"

"Let's not, Dad," I said.

"No, no, one job at a time," agreed Dad.

Ethel glared at me. "Wimp," she muttered.

I wanted to nip her ear.

"Right, follow me," commanded Dad. "I know a spot where the ground's a bit softer."

We padded along the hedgerows until we reached the wire fence of the farm. There, among a jumble of other buildings, stood the place we were making for.

The henhouse. I shivered with excitement.

"Right, before we start, what can you smell now?" said Dad.

For some time, I'd been aware of a strong and dangerous scent blowing towards us.

"Is that dog?" I asked.

Dad nodded.

"Now, cubs, do you think they can smell us?"

I looked at Elfreda and she looked back at me. Neither of us said anything.

Dad sighed. "Has it all gone in one ear and out the other?"

"No!" said Ethel. "They can't smell us because the wind's blowing their scent towards us, but our scent away from them."

"Very good, Ethel. I'm glad *one* of you was listening."

Ethel looked smug.

"But Dad," I said, "isn't it going to take us a long time to dig under that henhouse thing?"

"Good point, son. It would if we were starting from scratch, but I'm taking you to one of my tunnels. When I'm on my own I always stop and fill it in. The humans never seem to find it – I don't think they're very bright. There'll be no time to do that tonight, so I won't be able to use that one again."

"Oh do hurry, dear," whispered Mum. "I don't like all this hanging around."

"Your mother's right. Swift and silent, only one bird each. No sense being greedy."

"Like Uncle Percy," put in Elfreda.

"Well, Percy wasn't exactly greedy," said Dad, "but he didn't use his brains. If you come across a rabbit burrow full of nice fat bunnies, it makes sense to kill the lot, 'cos you can keep going back till you've emptied the burrow and filled your larder. That's what any right-thinking fox would do. But you can't do that with a barn full of chickens or you'll end up like Percy – nailed to the barn door by his tail. Are you listening *now*, Ethel?"

Ethel nodded like mad. She obviously didn't want to end up like Uncle Percy.

"Oh, please!" said Mum, hopping from paw to paw.

"All right, all right," said Alfred. "So – one kill each. Go straight for the neck and they won't even know it. Now get digging."

In no time at all we'd dug a shallow hole and scrabbled under the fence. Then with a sniff and a quick glance round we ran over to the barn.

Dad was right. It was easy to clear out his secret passageway, but it was pitch black and stuffy down there. I was glad when I saw the dim light that told us we were nearly through. Suddenly Ethel stopped short just in front of me and I bumped my nose against her bottom.

Dad had climbed out. "Now listen," he whispered into the tunnel. "Once the hens know we're here, they'll create such a racket they'd be heard in a thunderstorm. So *we* must act like lightning. Grab one and streak back under the fence as quick as you can. Then back to the wood, sticking to the hedgerows. Understand?"

Ethel crawled out next and I heaved myself up after her. I gasped. I didn't know there were that many chickens in the whole world! Then my mouth started to water. It couldn't be easier. There they all were, bedded down in their straw, just waiting for us. White ones, golden ones, speckled brown ones, feathers fluffed up and dreaming sweetly. One hen clucked softly in its sleep. Elfreda shoved me from behind and I shuffled forward.

Once Mum was through we all looked to Dad for the signal.

"Now!" he said, and we pounced!

The screeching and flapping of wings that followed nearly deafened me. Then my jaws closed round a feathery neck and I felt it break. But in that moment my eyes met the terror-stricken eyes of another hen.

"Help!" it shrieked.

I almost dropped my chicken. Once again, a picture of the sobbing rabbit flashed into my mind. But there was no time to think now, and the taste of blood had woken something in me. The foxiest bit of my brain told me to hold on and get out of there.

I dived for the tunnel but then, even before my front paws touched the ground…time stopped. My heart lurched.

A new sound had joined the squawks and shrieks. A deep-throated baying, then a long drawn-out howl…it was the dogs!

CHAPTER FOUR

The Nightmare Dog

My mind went blank. Blind panic gripped me.

"Listen!" hissed Dad through a mouthful of hen. "Don't worry. Just follow me and hang on to your chickens."

Somehow we all scrambled back through the tunnel. Once we were outside the henhouse we dashed across to the farm fence. I kept tripping over the body dangling from my mouth, but we made it! Under the wire we squeezed, Dad first, then Ethel, me and...

Like something out of a nightmare, a huge black creature came bounding round the corner with its jaws gaping wide. A low growl rumbled in its throat and its broken leash flapped as it ran.

It lunged at Elfreda.

Mum dropped her hen and flew at the dog's throat. She couldn't get a good grip, but she did knock it sideways.

"Quick, Elfreda!" yelled Dad.

No good. She crouched, stock still, staring straight ahead.

I was squeezing under the fence when suddenly something hot bubbled up inside me. How dare it! How dare it attack Mum and Elfreda! I wriggled back, leapt at the dog's hind legs, sank my teeth into one and hung on.

The dog threw its head back and howled, and Mum pushed Elfreda through the hole. Then she whipped round, ears flat and nose wrinkled in a menacing snarl.

The dog shook its leg violently, but my teeth were firmly clamped to it. I wasn't sure how long I could hold on though. Everything was spinning. I caught a glimpse of my sisters watching horror-struck through the fence. Then all I could see were yellow fangs and a great red tongue… A wave of hot stinking breath made me gag… I had to let go!

Mum leapt up and sank her teeth into its ear.

It howled again, and rolled over, trying to knock her off. It almost rolled on top of her, but she dodged out of the way. And again it rolled…towards the fence!

"Now!" yelled Dad, and Mum and me both leapt at the hole. Mum shoved me through and dived after me. She was almost through when the dog lunged at her and grabbed the end of her tail.

A high-pitched scream split the air as she tore herself away. But her tail…the beautiful white tip of her tail! Dripping with blood, it hung limply from the dog's fangs.

"Run!" ordered Dad, and we all pelted across the field.

I felt light-headed. My breath came in gasps. I could hear Mum beside me, whimpering with pain, and there was Dad ahead, chicken dangling from his mouth. Ethel was on his heels, dragging a hen almost as big as she was. What had happened to *my* chicken? I couldn't remember. And – where was Elfreda? I glanced back and saw her stumbling along with a dazed expression on her face, and beyond that…

I froze.

The dog was digging to make the hole bigger, and trying to

squeeze itself under the fence. Its nose was through, and its front paws. It twisted its head frantically from side to side and then its ears were through!

More dogs came bounding into the yard, baying and snarling.

"Dad!" I cried.

"Wouldn't you know it!" muttered Dad, and finally dropped his chicken. "Get to the river, quick!"

He fell back and picked Elfreda up by the scruff of her neck, just like he used to when we were tiny.

I didn't know how I reached the water. I felt as if someone else must have taken over my body and made my legs work, even though they had no strength left. I daren't look back, but I was dimly aware that the barking was growing fainter, until I could barely hear it over the pounding in my ears.

I fell into the shallows and waded downstream behind the others. Elfreda's paws and tail trailed in the water as she dangled from Dad's jaws. She was still alive, wasn't she?

At last Dad climbed the opposite bank and we all dragged ourselves up after him. Soaking wet and shivering, legs shaking and threatening to give way, I limped back to the earth.

Not till we reached home did my legs finally buckle under me. I found myself somehow nestling against a warm, panting body with a wonderful safe familiar smell. Although, there was another, sour smell mixed with it and I realised that Mum was licking the blood from the end of her tail.

"Poor Mum," I murmured, and watched half asleep as Dad laid Elfreda down beside me. She was wriggling and whimpering softly. Good, she'd be all right then… I could go to sleep…

"Ha! Did it!"

I jerked awake. Couldn't Ethel leave me in peace for once? What was that soggy bundle by her paws? Surely she hadn't managed to hang on to her chicken all the way home?

She had. It had lost its head and one wing, and the other wing was hanging off.

"Supper!" she said proudly.

Dad shook his head and laughed.

"Whistling worms, Ethel! You're amazing," he said.

Then he looked at me. "You too, son. Whoever would have thought it? You're a hero!"

Ethel gazed at me coolly.

"Yeah," she said, "p'raps you're not a wimp after all."

CHAPTER FIVE

The Autumn Offering

Soon everybody in the wood knew about our adventure. We had to tell and retell the story so many times, first to our cousins the Bushytails and then to our friends in the Badger Clan, and then… even the Great Stag heard about it!

Of course, I had to act all modest and say, "Oh, it was nothing really. *Anyone* would have turned back to join the fight." But I couldn't help feeling a bit proud of myself when Elfreda told everyone that I'd helped to save her life. And when the Great Stag himself called, with his Lady Hind, to congratulate me…

"Well done, young Sharpeyes, well done indeed," said the Stag, while I looked at the ground, and the whole family bowed low in front of him.

That summer was great, racing round enjoying ourselves. We were growing up, starting to look like proper foxes, copper-coloured on top and white underneath and on the tips of our tails. All our noses, ears and paws were black. All except for me. As that pesky rabbit had noticed, one of my paws was white.

Ethel called me the odd fox out, but Dad said it was a mark of distinction in the Sharpeyes family. His grandfather had had one white paw and had been noted for his wisdom and courage.

"Wisdom?" said Ethel. "Huh! Don't see much sign of that in Edgar!"

I only had one problem. Food.

It was solved quite soon after the raid, when Mum served us a quick lunch of wormburgers.

"Boring!" said Ethel. "I can catch worms for myself."

"Don't turn your nose up at a good source of protein," said Mum. "Foxes have always eaten worms when they can't get anything else."

Worms. They didn't seem to live in families. I couldn't imagine a worm crying for its mum. They probably had quite nice lives, wriggling around in the ground, and I'd like it if they could carry on doing it. But I had to eat something!

"I love wormburgers!" I said to Mum. "Can you teach me how to make them?"

She laughed. "You are funny, Edgar. Of course I can. It's easy."

Soon, most of my meals were wormburgers plus whatever leaves or baked roots the rest of them were eating.

Eggs were another lifesaver. After all, eggs weren't exactly alive. I felt a bit sorry for the parent birds, but I tried not to think about that.

Gradually the days grew shorter and berries began to ripen. Mum's wounded tail healed, though it had lost most of its white tip. We were expected to help find food now, and I tried to stop thinking about small animals being clan-folk. But I couldn't. Once or twice I caught a frog. I knew they didn't live in families and just grew from spawn, but I wasn't very happy about it. A frog definitely seemed more like a normal animal than a worm. But if Mum and Dad noticed that I never ever brought home a rat, mouse or vole, let alone a rabbit, they didn't say anything.

"You could eat nuts, like squirrels," said Elfreda, trying to be helpful.

Ethel fell about laughing. "Nuts for a nutcase!" she cackled.

That evening at supper, Mum had a surprise for us – a special autumn treat. It was a dish of deep purple fruit, stewed in its own juice and topped with a mix of crushed hazelnuts and sweet chestnuts – blackberry crumble. I thought it was the most delicious thing I'd eaten in my life.

"Autumn's a good time of year," said Dad, licking purple juice from round his mouth. "There's plenty of food around now, but it won't be so easy in a month or two. That's why we have the Festival."

"Yeah, we know about that," said Elfreda. "The Autumn Offaling, or something."

Mum laughed. "Offering, not offaling, because we offer up gifts to say thank you for all our good food and to ask for food in the winter."

"Who do we ask?" I said.

"The Stag, of course," said Dad. "But he's just a stand-in for a higher power."

"What higher power?" said Ethel. "There's nobody higher than the Stag."

"That's where you're wrong," said Mum. "One day the Stag will die, but the world will go on turning. We'll still have spring, summer and autumn, when food's easy to find, and winter when it's hard."

"So first we have the ceremony, the serious bit of the Festival," said Dad, "then when that's over we can get down to the feasting and games and all that."

"And during the ceremony you've each got to make a presentation to the Stag and his Lady," said Mum. "Something nice to eat. Everybody's got to. The squirrels bring little baskets of nuts, the hedgehogs bring bowls of worms and slugs, the rabbits bring herbs and vegetables and *we've* got to take the sort of thing *we* usually eat. And remember – there's no killing for three days once the Festival's started, so you've got to get it ready in plenty of time. Then we share it all around."

"Share it round?" said Ethel. "Yuk! I'm not going to eat any of that muck that rabbits and squirrels eat!"

"Don't be stupid, Ethel," said Mum. "Obviously we share it among our own kind. Otherwise you'd get rabbits sitting around eating bits of their dead relatives!"

Ethel and Elfreda giggled.

"Oh, do try a bit of Grandma's leg," said Ethel in a silly voice. "It's absolutely delicious!"

"Uncle Henry tastes wonderful in a stew!" said Elfreda. "It's a shame he can't be here to enjoy it with us!"

They fell around laughing, but I didn't join in.

The whole wood was throbbing with excitement, as everyone scurried around finding their own offering, and trying not to be turned into someone else's offering.

I didn't know what to take. Eggs? It was too late in the year to find any. Wormburgers? They didn't seem special enough.

Then I remembered Mum's blackberry crumble. Perfect! I didn't think I could make a crumble, but I could collect blackberries. I didn't tell the others – everyone wanted their gift to be a surprise. Mum and Dad had helped us weave some baskets, and we half-filled them with grass and leaves.

The day before the ceremony, I crept off to a bramble hedge and filled my basket with glossy, juicy blackberries (eating as much as I put inside). Then I washed the juice off my face and paws, covered the berries with leaves, stole home and hid the basket under fern from my mattress.

The next morning dawned cool and clear, and we washed and brushed ourselves extra carefully. We gripped our baskets between our teeth and waited outside the earth.

"Let's have a look at you," said Dad, eyeing us up and down. "Very smart!"

"I think we should just check their offerings," said Mum.

"No!" shouted Ethel and Elfreda, flinging themselves on their baskets. "It's a secret! It's a surprise!"

Dad laughed. "Don't be such a worryguts! Don't you remember when we were cubs? Everyone wants to keep their offering a secret."

Mum looked at me, opened her mouth to say something, then shut it again.

"Don't worry, Mum," whispered Elfreda. "I bet he's got a pile of wormburgers in there."

"He can share them with the hedgehogs," muttered Ethel.

I smiled to myself. Wait till they saw what I'd really got.

Then we all trooped off to the dell in the middle of the wood.

There stood the Great Stag and his Lady, surrounded by hundreds of animals, large and small, and all completely silent. Somewhere, somebody giggled and was hushed.

I looked shyly at the Hind. Beneath her crown of acorns and berries her eyes were gentle and kind. She might be the Lady of the Wood, but she seemed like the sort of animal you could tell your troubles to. Then I looked at the Stag. No crown there. He didn't need one with his magnificent antlers. And no kindly expression in his eyes. No expression at all as far as I could see. I shivered.

The ceremony began. It seemed to take a hundred years, but at last it was our turn.

"Welcome, Family Sharpeyes," said the Stag. "We are pleased, Hilda, that you have recovered so well from your unfortunate accident at the farm. And what have you all brought for the festivities?"

Dad cleared his throat.

"If it please your grace, a pheasant."

The Stag nodded.

"And I have brought a rabbit," said Mum.

"Two rats," said Elfreda.

"Four field mice," said Ethel.

"And our hero Edgar," smiled the Hind, "what have you brought for the feast?"

"Some blackberries," I said.

In the silence that followed, you could have heard an acorn drop.

At last the Hind spoke.

"That is an unusual offering for a fox," she said gently.

"Unusual is a mild word," said the Stag. "Surely you do not expect us to accept this?"

He stared down at me and waited.

My mouth felt dry as a fallen leaf. This wasn't happening – how had things suddenly gone so wrong? I wished I were anywhere in the world but here, with hundreds of eyes trained on me, and hundreds of ears waiting for me to speak.

"But, but I love blackberries," I whispered.

"You may love them, but could you live on them?"

I didn't say anything, so the Stag went on.

"Blackberries are an autumn treat, and many here would be glad to share them with you. Indeed, our friends the birds have gathered basketfuls of berries for us. But feasting is not the main purpose of our ceremony, as you know."

The Stag paused and looked around at the gathering of woodland creatures.

"We are met here to give thanks for the gifts of summer and autumn, and to ask for strength to survive the coming winter. We bring what is necessary for our survival, Edgar, you know that, not sweet things that we can do without. It is too late now for you to bring a proper offering. No creature may be killed for the next three days. Of course you may stay and take part in the festivities, but we cannot accept your blackberries."

He looked gravely at me, and I wished I could burrow into the carpet of leaves and hide myself. But I couldn't do that. What *should* I do? Apologise and take my basket away, I supposed... but...it wasn't fair. It just wasn't fair!

"But I hate killing!" I burst out. "Why do foxes have to kill to eat? Other animals don't. I want to be *friends* with rabbits and field mice and voles, not eat them! I'm sure I could get used to eating nuts, or I could eat vegetables, like rabbits. Why is a dead animal the only proper offering?"

I heard a gasp...silence...then a growing buzz of conversation.

"Disgraceful!" said an old dog-fox.

"Sounds all right to me," whispered a tiny voice nearby.

"We could do with a few more like him," muttered a small voice on my other side.

"Trouble'll come of this, mark my words," growled the slow, deep voice of the Chief of the Badger Clan. "Arguing with the Great Stag! This'll bring bad luck, see if it doesn't."

"Silence!" thundered the Stag. "Listen, oh creatures, to my

words. This was no mistake then, but deliberate defiance! Never in my time, or my father's or grandfather's time, has an animal gone against nature like this. For thousands of years we have obeyed the laws of nature, and for a very good reason. It is the only way to live and be happy in this world. The only creature who has not obeyed these laws is that traitor – man. He has cast himself out from our ways and is busy trying to ruin our beautiful earth.

"You are young, Edgar, but not too young to know what you are doing. Indeed, you are old enough to find food for yourself, or I would not say what I am about to say."

He paused, then slowly and clearly intoned these words:

"Be outcast from your family and our community, Edgar Sharpeyes, for a year from today. Depart from our wood alone, until you have learnt the truth – a fox cannot live on food proper to other creatures. Your family must stay here without you. Come back in a year, with the correct offering, and we will accept you once more. You may say goodbye to your family now, and then – be gone!"

CHAPTER SIX

Goodbyes

What?... But... No! This wasn't happening! I stood, stunned, unable to believe what I'd just heard. There must be some mistake. Then I heard Mum give a low moan and saw Elfreda fling herself at the Stag's hooves. It *was* happening.

"Oh, please don't!" cried Elfreda. "Edgar saved my life. Oh, please let him off!"

The Stag stood as if he were made of stone.

"I have spoken," he said.

Dad nudged my shoulder.

"Come on, son," he muttered. "Don't make it worse. If you say anything else he might never let you come back."

Suddenly I couldn't bear it. With a wild sweep of my head I knocked my basket over and shot off towards home. I ran and ran, through the crowds, between the trees, all the way back to the earth. Then I flung myself down on the ground outside and sobbed.

After a while, when I hadn't got any sobs left, I became aware of familiar black paws all around me. Then a nose rubbed mine and Dad's voice said, "Now, son, this won't make things any better."

I just lay there and shut my eyes again. Then it was Ethel's voice.

"You've always got to be the odd fox out, haven't you?" she said.

"Oh, Ethel, how can you say such a thing?" That was Mum. "As if he did it on purpose!"

The voices floated round over my head, and seemed to have nothing to do with me.

"Look," Dad again, "why don't you two go back and join the party? Your mother and I can get Edgar sorted out."

"Oh no," wailed Elfreda, "not without Edgar!"

Suddenly her head was burrowing into my side and she was sobbing just as violently as I had been a few minutes before.

"Don't, Elfreda, don't," I murmured and licked her face. Then I sat up shakily and looked round at the other three.

"I'm sorry," I mumbled, "I'm so sorry. I had no idea I'd cause all this trouble."

Mum and Dad sat down facing me. Ethel moved a bit away and lay looking in the opposite direction.

"But…whistling worms, son, what made you do it?" Dad shook his head. "It's my fault. I should have let your mother check your baskets."

"No," said Mum, "I should have insisted."

Dad stood up again and started pacing around.

"I can't have brought you up properly. I haven't explained things to you clearly enough – the ways of the wild, and all that."

"No, Dad, it's not your fault!" I cried. "It's me – there's something funny about me. I was just born different or something."

"Well, when you've all stopped blaming yourselves," said Ethel, turning round, "I'd like to say that I don't blame myself in the slightest. I've always told Edgar he was acting dopey."

"And you weren't born different," sniffed Elfreda. "You were just like us till that day you came back and you didn't want any rabbit stew. Something happened that day, didn't it?"

Slowly I let all the breath out of my body. "Oh, I can't tell you. It sounds so stupid."

Mum gazed at me and her amber eyes looked as if they were trying to peer into my mind.

"You've got to, Edgar. We've got to lose you for a while, it seems, though I can't bear to think about it. But I'm not letting you go till I know what this is all about."

I sighed again, hesitated, and then let it all out in a rush. "Well, I met a rabbit, and once I'd talked to it, and realised that rabbits were clan-folk like us, I didn't want to eat it."

Silence. The whole family stared at me open-mouthed.

Then, "Oh, that's what all that 'rabbits are clan-folk' stuff was about," said Elfreda.

Ethel jumped up and thrust her nose into my face, making me shrink back.

"Listen, bozo!" she said. "You meet a rabbit, you don't go, 'Hi, nice weather we're having!' You meet a rabbit, you go – SNAP! End of rabbit, end of conversation!"

I blinked.

At last Mum spoke. "Of course rabbits are clan-folk, Edgar, but that doesn't mean we can't eat them. It's nature. They were given vegetables and grass to eat, and we were given small animals to eat. They know that, and if they're clever they can escape us. That's why they have such big families, Edgar. If we didn't eat some of them, the whole wood'd be overrun with rabbits."

My eyes opened wide in horror. I hadn't thought of that. So killing and blood were a necessary part of things?

"Then I don't think the world was very well planned!" I burst out.

"I'm beginning to think the Great Stag has a point, son," said Dad. "Perhaps you *do* need to go and learn the hard way that foxes have to kill to eat. Anyway," he sighed, "we don't have any choice. Come on, Edgar, let's get you sorted out."

And we all trailed inside, except Ethel. I turned back to her, but she ignored me and lay gazing grumpily at her front paws.

The rest of the day was spent preparing for my journey. Mum gave me some food in a leather bag: pickled pheasants' eggs, shelled hazelnuts, elderberries and blackberries, all wrapped in big leaves, plus a flask of water.

"I'd like to give you a crumble, dear, but it'd be a bit messy to carry."

She made me some mushroom nuggets too.

"Can't I put just a little bit of minced vole in? It does make it tastier."

"No, really, Mum, don't."

Gradually, I found myself getting involved in the preparations. Having something to do certainly took your mind off the way you were feeling. And after a while, Ethel sidled in and started to help.

Once the food was sorted out, Dad said, "Now sit down, son, and listen carefully. Your mother and I have been talking, and this is what we think. You're to go to Brock Wood and find the Keenears family. It's a good way off, but we'll tell you how to get there."

"My last name was Keenears before I married your father," said Mum. "My family moved to Brock Wood before you were all born, but I stayed here because of Alfred. I just know they'll make you welcome."

Then I had to memorise the way to Brock Wood. It was straightforward enough – except for one thing. Before I reached there, I had to cross something called the death-strip.

Mum shuddered when it was mentioned.

"It's why we don't visit them now," she said. "It wasn't so bad at first, but then those humans made it wider and the things go so fast… Oh, Alfred, do you think it's a good idea?"

"What things?" I asked.

"Zoom-hounds, son," said Dad. "And thunder-monsters. And, no, I don't think it's a good idea, but it's the only idea we've got."

"Zoom-hounds?" I whispered. "Thunder-monsters?"

"We call them that because of the noise they make," said Dad. "At least, that's the noise they make when they're racing along the death-strip. You see them sometimes on other paths, or going to and from the farm. They're not quite so noisy then."

"It was a lot better in the middle of the night," said Mum. "You remember that time we went?"

"That's exactly what I was thinking!" said Dad. "You must travel by night anyway, son, but especially when you're crossing the death-strip. Wait until the dead of night and only cross to the middle when you can't see any lights at all on that side."

"Lights?" I said.

"The zoom-hounds have bright lights that shine in the dark," explained Mum, "so at least you can see them coming."

"Then wait in the middle," said Dad. "There's a bit of ground you can stand on and a fence you can crawl under. Wait there till you can't see any lights on *that* side. Understand? Then you run the last bit and you're home and dry."

"If only it were that easy," said Mum.

"Oh, he'll be all right!" said Dad. "He's a sensible lad – in *most* ways." He glared at me for a moment, then shook himself. "If he follows our instructions, he'll be fine, and we'll see him next year when he's learned some sense.

"I'd come with you, son, but the Stag made it pretty clear you had to go on your own."

I nodded. "I know."

"Then there's nothing left but to say goodbye."

And that's when it really hit me. I'd been listening to instructions, taking them in, as if they were for some other animal. But that bag of provisions was for *me*. I stared in disbelief around my home, at the faces of my family. I had to leave them!

I wanted to scream, to cry, to attack somebody, to collapse in a heap, to be a baby cuddled up to Mum and Dad, never to leave their side!

But I had to go. You couldn't disobey the Stag. So now I struggled with tears, and tried to find voice enough to say goodbye.

"You are weird, Edgar," said Ethel, "but you're not a wimp. I think that old Stag's mean."

"I hate him!" spat Elfreda. "I'd like to... I'd like to... I don't know what I'd like to do to him, but something really horrible!"

"There's no point talking like that," said Dad. "His word's the law and that's all there is to it."

"Can't I go with him, Dad, just to the edge of the wood?" begged Elfreda. "I'll be very careful."

"I'm not sure, but – oh, I don't see why not. Well...come on then."

One by one, we climbed the entrance tunnel and went out into the evening. Then we nuzzled and rubbed faces for so long that I wondered if I'd have any face left.

"Good luck, son," whispered Dad.

"Yes, good luck," said Ethel.

Mum just went on stroking the side of my nose with her own. Finally she mumbled, "Remember me to my family…and take care, Edgar, take care."

"I will, Mum, don't worry." I swallowed hard. "Bye then."

And I turned and loped off into the wood without looking back.

CHAPTER SEVEN

Aidan

Elfreda followed me.

"Listen, Edgar," she said as we trotted through the trees. "There must be some way we can keep in touch. You know, send each other messages or something."

"Yeah, but how?" I said.

We loped on for a while in silence. Perhaps it was the fresh night air or perhaps it was Elfreda padding along beside me, but my spirits started to lift a bit. Maybe we *would* be able to keep in touch. And it was Mum's relations I was going to. Surely they'd be as nice as her. I tried to imagine Mum and Dad if some unknown cousin turned up at the earth. I knew they'd make him feel one of the family.

"How far are you going to come?"

"Well, not too far, after what the Stag said. Look, we *must* get this message thing sorted out."

But neither of us had any ideas.

Before long we left the wood and reached a huge oak tree in the middle of a field.

"We could scratch messages for each other on the bark," suggested Elfreda.

"What, like two lines for 'I'm okay', and three for 'Help!'?"

"Well, we could work out a code."

"No point," I said. "We might as well agree to meet here every full moon."

"Yeah!" said Elfreda. "Let's do that!"

"There's just one little problem," I said. "I'd have to keep getting back across that death-strip thing. I don't fancy doing that too often."

Elfreda sank into gloom again, and we both sat in silence under the tree, thinking, thinking, and getting nowhere.

Then the quiet was broken by a rustle and a little thump as something landed on a branch above us. We hadn't heard anything coming so we looked up, startled. Two feathery feet with long claws were grasping the branch, and above them two enormous eyes glared down at us. The eyes were set in a round flat face with a fierce hooked beak. The beak opened and there was a soft tu-whoo. It was a tawny owl. He gazed steadily at us, turning his head first one way, then the other.

"What are you twooo doooing here, hoo-hoooo? Yoooo should be feasting, too troooo, too troooo. Not up to mischief, are yoooo?"

"No, but it's a long story," I sighed. "I've been sent away."

"Hoo-hoooo, you're young Sharpeyes, aren't yoooo? I heard about yoooo. I'll introduce myself, toooo – Aidan Hootingly-ffeatherclaw, of the Northumbrian Hootingly-ffeatherclaws, too troooo."

"Oh – right," I said, trying to look as if I'd heard of the Northumbrian Hootingly-ffeatherclaws.

"With twoooo small 'f's, of course," said Aidan.

"Of course," said Elfreda, though I was sure she had no idea what an 'f' was. At least, *I* hadn't.

"Quite a stir *yoooo* caused," Aidan went on. "What a to-doooo, what a to-doooo. Well, where are you off toooo?"

"To Brock Wood, to some of my mum's family. If they'll have me, with my funny ideas."

"Ooooh, I know some others with funny ideas, quite a fyoooo," and Aidan laughed gently.

"What do you mean?" I demanded.

But he wouldn't say any more.

"Owls keep their counsel, they doooo, they doooo," was all we could get out of him.

Then suddenly he hooted, "I've got a cousin in Brock Wood toooo, Benedict by name, too troooo, too troooo. If you need to send nyooooos to your family, he'll fly to my oak tree here for yoooo. Same goes for yoooo, Sharpeyes daughter. I don't mind visiting Benedict with nyooooos of yoooo."

We both leapt up.

"Oh thank you, that's brilliant!" I cried.

"That's just what we were talking about, how we were going to keep in touch, and we didn't know how," said Elfreda.

"It's like magic, as if you knew what we wanted," I said. "Are owls magic?"

"Hoo-hoooo," chuckled Aidan. "Owls keep their counsel, but they know a thing or twoooo. Good luck, young Sharpeyes. It's time I floooo."

And he swooped away.

"Goodbye! Goodbye and thank you!" we called after him, and then fell quiet again.

"I must be off as well," said Elfreda, shifting from one paw to the other.

"I know."

We looked awkwardly at each other.

"Are you going any further tonight?" Elfreda asked.

Suddenly I was absolutely exhausted.

"I'd better, I suppose – it's a bit open here."

"Come on, that hedge looks all right."

We padded across the field to a thick hawthorn hedge, and Elfreda helped me dig out a shallow hole to sleep in. It was partly under the hedge and partly in the open, but sheltered enough that no one was likely to see me.

"You'd better stay here most of tomorrow as well. It can't be far to the death-strip now, and you'll need to be *wide* awake to get across that. So get as much sleep as you can, right?"

I nodded. I could hardly keep my eyes open.

"Thanks for coming," I said.

"I'm glad you're properly grateful," grinned Elfreda.

Then she stood looking at the ground, looking at me, and then at the ground again.

"Well – I really must go."

But she didn't move.

"Oh, go on, Elfreda, please. You're only making it worse."

"Well – goodbye then, and good luck."

We nuzzled each other one last time, and Elfreda finally turned and loped away. I watched her growing smaller, until she melted into the night.

Then I looked up at the stars. The sky was so big. You weren't supposed to see stars when you were going to sleep. You were supposed to see your bedroom ceiling with the tree-roots poking through. And more than that, you were supposed to be curled up warm with your sisters, not all alone in an open field.

And perhaps your mum would come and tell you a story, even though you were getting big. A story about the Spring Hare.

I tried to curl myself into a comfortable position. If only the Spring Hare would come and help me now. But it was probably the wrong time of year.

CHAPTER EIGHT

The Death-strip

That night I had a strange and horrible dream.

The Great Stag loomed over me with a dead rabbit in his mouth. Chickens shrieked "Help!" just before I bit through their necks. A jeering weasel offered me two brimming cups of dark liquid.

"Which tastes better, Edgar, blood or blackberry juice?" he sneered.

The gentle-eyed Hind gazed at me sadly.

"Oh, Edgar, how could you?" she sighed.

Then her face turned into Mum's face.

"Oh, Edgar, how could you?" she sobbed.

And there was the Stag again. "Be outcast, Edgar Sharpeyes." His voice was cold and grim.

"I'm sorry, I'm sorry. I didn't mean it! I didn't want to cause trouble!"

I jumped, and realised that I'd been calling out in my sleep. I looked around in panic. Suppose someone had heard me! But no one else was around. Just me. All on my own.

It was the first time I'd woken up anywhere but in my own

bed in the earth, surrounded by my family. Big waves of loneliness crashed over me. I laid my nose on my front paws, and the world grew blurry as my eyes swam with tears.

The sun was low in the sky. Despite my bad dreams, I must have slept most of the day away. It was late afternoon – no wonder I was hungry! I brushed away my tears, opened my bag and ate three mushroom nuggets, a pickled egg and some elderberries. Then I drank nearly all the water. I was very thirsty and surely I'd soon find a stream where I could refill the flask.

With something in my stomach I cheered up a bit. After all, you couldn't have a better sister than Elfreda, and Aidan Hootingly-ffeatherclaw was going to help us keep in touch. It was dead lucky that he'd turned up just then!

So I sat up, repacked my bag and, as the sun was going down, set off once more on my journey.

According to Dad, I should have four more fields to cross before I reached the death-strip. What would it look like? Would I know what it was?

Soon I started to notice a strange humming noise, rather like a swarm of bees. The buzzing grew louder and deeper as I trotted on. It couldn't really be bees, could it? But what other creature made a noise like that? Perhaps it was coming from the death-strip itself!

Then the ground started to vibrate. I hardly noticed it at first – just a faint tremor tingling through my paws and up my legs. I strained to peer above the stubble in the field, but all I could see were more hedgerows.

By the time I reached the last field the noise was deafening, and the ground was shaking beneath my paws.

And now I could see what was causing it.

Zoom-hounds!

At that point I almost gave up and slunk back home. But how could I? With the Great Stag behind me and these creatures in front of me, where could I go? My legs went wobbly and I collapsed in a heap.

Zoom-hounds! Charging along at incredible speeds, chasing each other on weird round things, snarling as they ran. Could you call it running? They had no legs!

I could never have imagined anything like this. It was dark now, but I could still see them clearly. Their staring, brilliant eyes glared ahead, so bright that light shone out from them to dazzle their prey. A picture flashed into my mind, of me, helpless, caught in that glare, frozen and trapped.

But then – then, with a thunderous roar that left me in no doubt what it was, came a vast, hideous monster, belching smoke and making the ground shudder. Then came another, and another. A family of thunder-monsters!

I sat stunned in the middle of the field. How could I go on? But I had to. So I sprawled on my belly and slowly wriggled forward. When I reached the fence that separated the field from the death-strip, I poked my nose underneath and just lay there.

I was supposed to cross that?

Mum and Dad had said it'd be almost empty in the middle of the night. How did they know? Had they got it right? Well, there was nothing I could do but lie there and wait.

The stink was overpowering. No animal I'd ever met had breath that smelt that bad. Not even the dog at the farm. I had to keep shifting myself as thistles pricked my tummy and nettles tickled my nose. And still the creatures stampeded on.

The thunder-monsters were the worst. I'd never imagined anything so massive, so menacing. Where did they live? They seemed to travel in families. There must be a terrifying land somewhere filled with monster-lairs. I shut my eyes and covered my ears with my paws when another three roared by together.

At last – I couldn't tell how long I'd been lying there, except that the moon was now high in the sky – I thought there seemed to be bigger gaps between the zoom-hounds. Gradually the noise was growing quieter, though sometimes I shot in the air when one of them whizzed past.

Finally, there was a short space of time with nothing at all on my side of the death-strip. Then a zoom-hound raced by and I realised that I'd have to take my chance. This might be the only quiet bit of the night. It could be now or never.

So I wriggled under the fence and waited. Nothing. There was nothing coming! I gulped in some air, held my breath and sped across to the fence in the middle.

Success!

I was halfway there!

I rested a minute, till my heart had stopped thumping quite so hard, and crawled under the bottom bar of the fence.

A zoom-hound zipped by and the thrum gradually faded into the distance. Then silence again.

Come on! I said to myself. What are you waiting for?

This time I took several deep breaths, crouched and bounded on to the death-strip.

There was an earsplitting bellow... Panic!... Should I carry on or go back?

Too late.

The creature caught me in the glare of its brilliant eyes and I found that I couldn't move...everything slowed down... I watched in horror as it glided towards me.

It was just like the picture that had flashed through my mind, and there was nothing I could do.

Slam!!

I was flying!

I hit the ground with a bone-crunching thud and blackness smothered everything.

CHAPTER NINE

That Rabbit Again

The darkness was complete. I knew nothing. Then, as if from far away, I heard a voice.

"Are you a'right? Fox-face, are you a'right?"

The voice dragged me out of the black pit I'd been lying in, and I started to hear other noises. Zoom, growl, rumble – only a few fox-lengths away from me.

"Wake up, Fox-face, wake up!"

I half opened my eyes. It was light – the sort of grey light you get when the sun's coming up. There was something swimming around in the air above me – a black twitchy nose, two gleaming brown eyes and two long grey-brown ears. They danced around so that sometimes the nose was on top and sometimes the ears. Then they doubled up and became four eyes, four ears and two noses. I gave up trying to make sense of it and closed my eyes again.

But I'd seen those eyes before, hadn't I?...and heard that voice...somewhere...and smelt that warm, interesting smell...a long time ago...

"Wake up, Foxy!" the creature began again. "D'you remember me?"

I tried again, and this time the face stayed in focus. But where was I? How did I get here? And who was this animal?

"Look, we oughtta get you further behind this bush."

I felt two paws pushing my hind quarters. I moaned, but didn't move.

"Yo, Fox, you have to help as well, you know," the voice went on crossly. "Don't you remember me? I know it's you. There ain't that many foxes around with one white paw. I did my rap for you. D'you remember?"

Suddenly everything jumbled back into my brain – talking to the rabbit, the Autumn Offering, the Great Stag, the journey... and the death-strip.

"Oh, it's you," I groaned. "Well, you're doing it again, aren't you, talking to a fox."

"Yeah, but you didn't hurt me before and, to be honest, you ain't lookin' too dangerous at the moment."

My head was thumping, my ribs were aching and one of my front legs was hurting badly. But I was awake.

"It's all your fault, you know. All this is your fault," I mumbled. "If it weren't for you I'd be at home now, enjoying myself, leading a normal life."

"What d'you mean?" The rabbit sat up indignantly. "Fox, it's *your* fault, for not usin' the tunnel. You're lucky to be alive at all, tryin' to cross the death-strip. I didn't think you were that bright before, and it looks like I was right!"

"Tunnel? What are you talking about?"

I struggled to lift my head and for the first time really looked at the rabbit. He was a lot bigger – already almost a full-grown buck – but, yes...it was the same cocky creature I'd talked to all those moons ago.

"Duh! The tunnel! Look! It's only just over there, slugbrain

– the death-strip tunnel! Some humans dug it so that us animals could cross the death-strip without bein' flattened by a thunder-monster."

I groaned again. "Mum and Dad didn't tell me about that. They can't have known."

"Well, I s'pose it's fairly new. If they haven't been in these parts for a while they wouldn't know about it," said the rabbit. "But look, how we gonna get you away from here? Can you stand up?"

I tried, but my head swam and a sharp pain shot through my front leg. I sank down, defeated.

"I'm so thirsty," I said.

"Oh right, this is yours, ain't it?" said the rabbit, taking a leather flask out of a bag. "I think there's some water in it."

I opened my mouth, and the rabbit held the flask upside down over it. A few drops of water trickled out on to my parched tongue. If only I'd saved some more!

"Can you lean on me? Give it a try."

Once more I struggled to get up and lean against the rabbit, but it was no good. I was too heavy and we both toppled over.

"I'll have to git Harold," said the rabbit. "He'll do it."

"I don't think even two rabbits'll be strong enough," I said.

"Oh, Harold ain't a rabbit, he's a badger. What's your name, anyway, Fox-face? I'm Robbo Twitchnose, known to my fans this side of the strip as *the* Rappin' Rabbit."

Despite everything, I managed a smile.

"Pleased to meet you, Robbo. I'm Edgar Sharpeyes."

Robbo held out a paw, and I shook it with my good front paw.

"Now let's git you hidden. A bit more co-operation this time please. We need to git you right behind that bush."

Robbo pushed, and I painfully shuffled until I was quite out of view of the death-strip monsters.

"Right. Now don't move. I'll be back."

I was beginning to warm to him, and I didn't feel like being left alone again so soon.

"I liked your rap," I said. "How did it go?"

Looking not at all sorry to give a performance, Robbo sat up, thumped his back paw on the ground, just as he had all those moons ago, and chanted:

"Close to home or wand'rin' far,
Remember this rap wherever you are:
Owl or hawk,
Don't stop to talk, bro.
Weasel or stoat,
They'll be at your throat, bro.
Fox or crow,
You'd better just go-go.
Dog or man,
Escape if you can, yo.
A-*one* and a-*two* and a-three four *five*,
This is the rap that'll keep you ALIVE."

"Yeah, I like that," I said. "You could add some more lines to it. I can't think of anything to rhyme with monster, but how about:

If you see a zoom-hound,
Don't stick around."

"Hm," grunted Robbo. "I'll think about it."

"You know what," I said, "you still aren't thinking about the meaning of your rap, are you?"

"What d'you mean?"

"Well, talking to foxes. You couldn't be sure I was the one you met before, and you won't find many foxes around like me."

"Huh," grunted Robbo again. "Think you know everythin', don't ya. Now don't you move from there."

As if I could.

And Robbo hopped off to find Harold.

Safe behind the bush I tried to doze, but my mouth was so dry and my head was throbbing worse than ever. An irritating fly kept buzzing round and I didn't have the energy to shoo it away. I was still too close to those zoom-hounds as well and there were more and more of them zooming by. Suppose one of them decided to come up on the grass after me?

The sun was getting higher now and I was grateful for the shade from the bush. It seemed more like summer than autumn. But where was that rabbit? Perhaps something had happened to him! Rabbits were always in danger, weren't they, much more than foxes. Perhaps another fox would get him and he'd never come back, and what would happen to me then? No one would know I was here and I'd get thirstier and thirstier until I died.

CHAPTER TEN

Badgers' Hollow

Animal voices! Gruff badger tones and a light rabbit voice were growing nearer and nearer. Relief flooded through me. And there was Robbo with not one badger but two. They were carrying a sort of mat of woven grasses stretched between two long sticks. With some difficulty and a lot of instructions from Robbo, the badgers heaved me on to it. When they'd carried me into a clump of trees about thirty fox-lengths from the road, they put the mat thing down.

"Now, my dear," said the elderly female badger, "I'm sure that this is what you really want."

She unstoppered an earthenware bottle slung round her tubby body and put it to my mouth. It was only water, but I thought I'd never in my life tasted anything so delicious. I would have carried on glugging it down until the bottle was empty, but the badger eased it away.

"Careful," she said. "We don't want you to be sick."

"Thank you," I gasped.

"And now we can introduce ourselves," said the other badger. "You must think we're very rude."

"Oh, no," I said.

"Yes, excuse our haste, my dear," said the first badger, "but we didn't like being in sight of those horrible zoom-hounds. They have humans inside them, you know. I'm Edith Greycoat, and this is my husband Harold."

Harold bowed and beamed at me.

"Pleased to meet you," I said. "Sorry – did you say the zoom-hounds have humans in them? Do they eat humans, then?"

Harold chuckled. "No, no. The humans make the zoom-hounds and travel round in them. Apparently their legs are so feeble they won't carry them very far, so they use these things instead. Quite clever, I suppose. You've got to give it to them. They make those thunder-monsters as well."

I shook my head. It was too much to take in.

"I thought the zoom-hounds were alive! I thought the thunder-monsters were real monsters!"

"It's an easy mistake to make, dear," smiled Edith, "and you might as well think of them as monsters, to remind yourself to stay well away from them."

I sank back on to the grass mat. The world was a stranger place than I'd imagined.

"I'm really grateful for all this," I said. "Where are you taking me?"

"Back to our sett, Edgar," said Harold. "Yes, Robert's told us…"

"Robbo!" interrupted the rabbit crossly. "Yo, Stripy, the name's Robbo!"

"And my name's Harold," said the badger tetchily. "Oh very well, *Robbo's* told us your name, and quite a bit about you, though there's a lot more we'd like to know."

"But not now, dear," said his wife. "We've a way to go, and the sooner we make him properly comfortable in bed, the better."

So we all set off once more, across fields and then through shrubby woodland, stopping now and again for a rest.

"It's a good thing you're not full-grown, young fox," puffed Harold, more than once. "You're quite heavy enough as it is."

"Oh, sorry," I said. "This thing's really useful, though, isn't it? What do you call it?"

"It's a stretcher," explained Edith, "and I'm not sure we could carry you at all without it."

The journey was painful. I seemed to be throbbing all over, but I took my mind off the aches and soreness by watching Robbo running about giving directions, as if the badgers didn't know the way to their own sett.

At last we passed between two low hills into a grassy hollow, and then down a tunnel and into an underground chamber. What a relief, to be eased on to a comfortable fern bed in a home very like my own.

Edith gave me another drink of water, this time with a slightly bitter taste.

"It's willow bark for your aches and pains, dear. Now drink it up and have a good rest."

I drank it up and laid my head thankfully on a soft pillow made of something I didn't recognise... It was so warm...so cosy...so... I was asleep.

I was woken by the light of a small candle. Robbo had gone, but Harold and Edith were standing near my bed with another, younger badger.

"Sorry, my dear," said Edith, "did we wake you up? We've just brought our son-in-law Osbert along to have a look at you. He's very good with broken bones and things."

Osbert gently prodded and poked me, while I gritted my teeth and said the odd, "Ouch!"

Finally he declared, "It's not too serious. Your front leg's broken, but it's a clean break. Your ribs might be slightly cracked, or they might just be badly bruised. Either way, they'll heal if you're careful for a week or so. The rest is just bumps, bruises and shock. You're very lucky, young fox. That could have been the end of you."

He gently put my leg in a splint, and propped me up with some more of the soft white stuff.

"What *is* this?" I asked, stroking the pillow with my paw.

"Sheep's wool," said Harold. "Nothing but the best here. We gather it from the hedgerows."

Then Edith, who'd disappeared for a while, came back carrying a wooden bowl of steaming broth, balanced on a tray. I sniffed. It smelt good! My mouth started to water. I dipped my nose in. It tasted good! I was so hungry, I'd probably drink some of it anyway. But I had to know.

"Er, what's in this, if you don't mind my asking?"

"Just vegetables, dear. Come on now, it'll do you the world of good."

"No animals?" I asked.

The three badgers beamed all over their stripy faces.

"Goodness no, this is Badgers' Hollow," said Harold. "We don't eat other animals here. Everyone who lives here has to agree not to kill anyone else. I'm afraid if you do eat other creatures, Edgar, you'll have to move on once you're better. But I've a feeling you might think like us."

"Yes," nodded Osbert, "Robbo's told us all about how you wouldn't attack him when you were both little, how you wanted to be friends."

"So we're hoping," said Edith, "that you still feel the same way."

My jaw dropped open, and Edith grabbed the tray before it could fall on the floor.

"You mean," I gasped, "you don't – you don't eat animals at all?"

The badgers nodded and went on smiling.

"You mean…you mean I'm not mad?"

"What do you mean, Edgar? Who said you were mad?" asked Edith.

"The Great Stag! Well, he didn't exactly say I was mad. He said…he said you couldn't live on vegetables and things if you were a fox…or a badger, I suppose. Because I tried to give some blackberries at the Autumn Offering and he said…you mean…" deep breath, "Am I awake?"

They all laughed and told me that, yes, I was.

Slowly, slowly my astonishment turned to joy. An amazed smile spread over my face.

"Then I'm not alone? I'm not the only one who thinks like this? The Great Stag was wrong?"

The badgers nodded again.

"He said, never in his father's time or his grandfather's time had anyone tried to go against nature, except me."

"Stuff and nonsense," snorted Harold. "He's a bit too high and mighty, he is. He wouldn't be so keen on killing if there were still wolves and bears around, who could kill him."

"There are humans, dear," Edith reminded him.

"Yes, well, humans, they're something else, aren't they? None of us is safe from humans."

"Some humans did dig the death-strip tunnel, dear," said Edith.

"Hiccupping hedgehogs! I do wish you wouldn't keep interrupting!" tutted Harold. "You're getting me confused."

"Sorry, dear," said Edith, not looking at all sorry.

"All right," Harold went on. "Some humans do kill deer, and some humans do dig death-strip tunnels, but we're getting right away from the point here. The point is, the Great Stag knows jolly well about us in the Hollow, so what he said to Edgar wasn't strictly true."

Osbert nodded and joined in the conversation. "He doesn't like other animals knowing about us. The trouble with the Great Stag is, he's afraid of change."

"Drink your soup, dear, it's going cold," said Edith suddenly, and I obeyed as if I was in a dream.

"Now just you rest and get better," she went on. "There's been too much talking. Have another good sleep, and we can talk some more tomorrow."

The three badgers left me, but it was some time before I could get back to sleep. As I lay there in the dark, I almost forgot my aches and pains. My whole body seemed to overflow with this new feeling of delight.

I was not mad. I was not alone. There *were* other animals who thought like me.

CHAPTER ELEVEN

A Different World

Next morning, after breakfast, Edith poked her head into the bedroom.

"You've got a visitor," she said mysteriously. "And it's someone who looks a lot like you. Can you guess?"

I shook my head.

"It's Hugo – one of your cousins from your mother's family!"

A young fox bounded in and threw himself on to the end of the bed.

"Hello, cousin Edgar!" grinned Hugo. "Been trying to kill yourself, have you? You obviously don't get your brains from the Keenears side of the family!"

"Look, I didn't know about the tunnel, okay? I feel a right idiot with everyone going on about it."

"Oh, we like to make you feel welcome," said Hugo.

"But what are *you* doing here?" I said. "I was on my way to find all of you in Brock Wood when the zoom-hound got me. Mum said her family wouldn't mind me living with them after I got chucked out of Horn Wood."

"I *live* in the Hollow," said Hugo. "Didn't Edith tell you?"

"Hang on…you're a fox, right? And you live in Badgers' Hollow, so you don't eat animals?" I said, stupefied.

"Well, I think I'm a fox. I was the last time I looked," said Hugo, examining himself all over, and even turning round to try and look at his tail.

I laughed.

"And I definitely don't eat animals, or they'd chuck me out!"

He bounced on to the bed again.

I couldn't believe this.

"But what about the rest of your family?" I asked.

"Oh, they're normal. They still live in Brock Wood. I'm the weirdo. They don't seem to mind, though."

We worked out that Hugo was about two moons older than me – he was born just before the last Spring Festival, while me and my sisters were born just after it.

Hugo wanted to know all about his relations in Horn Wood, but I kept coming back to one thing. Why had Hugo decided not to eat animals?

"What made you feel like that?" I asked him. "I'm so used to being the odd fox out. I can't believe all this."

"Dunno, really," said Hugo. "I used to come and play here when I was little, and, well, I like it here. I'd rather be friends with rabbits and things than eat them. Robbo's a laugh, isn't he?"

"Yeah, why does he talk like that?" I said.

"I think it started in Horn Wood," shrugged Hugo, "with a group of rapping rabbits. Robbo brought it over here and now all the young rabbits do it. They think it's really cool."

"So you just decided to come and live here?"

"Yeah, 'cos when you *know* animals who don't eat other animals – I mean, animals like badgers, who usually *do* kill for food – it sort of makes you think about things… I still go back and see my family, of course. It's not far."

I was envious. I wished I could just pop back and visit *my* family.

"But what about the Brock Wood Great Stag?" I asked. "Didn't he kick up a fuss?"

"They don't have one. No deer at all, in fact."

"So who decides things?"

"Things mostly seem to run along pretty well on their own," said Hugo. "And if there *is* an important decision to take, they have a moot."

"A moot?"

"That's a sort of general discussion, and sometimes there's a vote."

I tried to imagine the Great Stag asking for a vote on anything, but I gave up.

"Then who takes charge at the Great Festivals?" I asked.

"The heads of the different clans take it in turn," said Hugo. "It seems to work all right. And Harold and Edith usually do that sort of thing here, just because they're the oldest. But they don't make a big deal out of it."

I shook my head.

"After all that stuff the Great Stag told me," I said. "It's like living in a different world over here."

I found out that the Hollow had been run by badgers in this peaceable way for a few years now, but that Hugo was the first fox to live there. He'd been followed by his cubhood friend Mildred Copperbrush. I soon realised that they were more than friends now. In fact they were planning to set up home together.

My next visitor was Robbo. Apparently he also had a girlfriend, and they'd just got engaged.

"Aren't you a bit young for that?" I asked.

"Oh, us rabbits don't hang around, y'know," said Robbo.

I started to feel that I was missing out on something.

"How did you get here, anyway, Robbo?" I asked. "It's a long way from Horn Wood."

"T'ain't that far," replied Robbo. "An' I'm a rollin' stone, always on the lookout for adventure. But this seemed a good place to put down some roots. I reckoned they could use a rabbit of my talents."

Then after lunch, yet more visitors came calling. It felt like the whole of Badgers' Hollow was trooping through my bedroom. One of them was Osbert, the badger who'd set my leg in a splint, and with him was a younger version of himself, carrying a basket of tiny dark red berries.

"Come to see how the patient's doing," said Osbert.

"I'm being really well looked after," I said. "Still a bit sore, but okay."

"Good, good," said Osbert. "I'd like you to meet my younger brother, Cuthbert. He lives next door."

"Hello, Edgar," said Cuthbert. "I've brought you some elderberries. They're leftovers from my wine-making. I'm sure Edith's stuffing you full of good things, but, well, you know, it's the thought that counts."

And he smiled such a friendly smile that I knew straight away we were going to get on.

"Oh, thank you. I love berries," I said.

"Yeah, we heard it was some blackberries got you chucked out of Horn Wood," grinned Cuthbert.

"Is there anything you lot *don't* know about me?" I asked.

Then Edith came bustling in to shoo them out.

"He needs a doze," she said firmly.

"Quite right, quite right," said Osbert, and I was left alone.

I lay for a while, feeling achy but contented and gradually slipped into a dream. A giant basket of blackberries was sitting in the middle of the death-strip and on the horizon appeared a zoom-hound with a stag's antlers sprouting from its top. Closer and closer it sped until… SMASH! It tore into the basket and fruit spilled everywhere. Then from both sides of the death-strip crept animals of all kinds to feast on the berries. "What a silly fruit basket," said a rabbit who looked just like Robbo. "It should have used the death-strip tunnel!" In my sleep I smiled.

After a few days in bed, I was well enough to get up and hobble round on three legs. Robbo's guided tour of Badgers' Hollow didn't take long. As well as the badgers and foxes I'd met, there were moles, hedgehogs, different kinds of mice and voles, a few squirrels and lots of rabbits.

In the centre was a grassy dell and around that rose a number of low mounds and a few trees. One of the mounds had been hollowed out and had little round holes as windows.

"Yo, this is the cheese room," said Robbo, ushering me inside.

I sniffed a strange scent, of smoke mixed with something I couldn't identify. In the middle of the room was a fire, smouldering very low, and on the fire was set a dish of some white stuff.

"What's that?" I asked.

"Cows' milk," said a young rabbit dipping her paw in. "I'm checking it's the right temperature."

"Not too hot, dear," warned an elderly rabbit sitting nearby with some leaves on her lap. These were bound together with long blades of grass, and she seemed to be piercing tiny holes in them with her claws. Was it my imagination or did she flinch when she saw me? But she quickly recovered herself.

"You must be Edgar," she smiled. "This is delicate work and they get torn so easily. But I've nearly finished this one."

I was mystified. What was she doing?

"This is Flopsy, cheese-maker-in-chief," said Robbo, waving his paw at the elderly rabbit. "An' *I'll* tell ya how ya make the cheese."

"Oh get lost, Robbo," said the young rabbit. "You think you know everything."

"An' this is my delightful fiancée Isabel Bobtail," said Robbo. "As polite an' friendly as ever."

Isabel ignored that and started to explain how to make cheese.

"You have to heat the milk but not boil it, then add some apple juice that's been sitting there a long time until it's sour and then you keep stirring the milk. Then you have to..."

By this time my head was spinning.

"And when it starts to look lumpy you pour it through these leaves with little holes into a dish. And then you... And then you... And you wrap the curds up in the leaves and it becomes cheese!"

"But whoever thought of something so complicated?" I asked, amazed.

"I learned it from humans," said Flopsy.

Now I was even more amazed.

"Humans?!" I gasped.

"Yes, we used to live with humans, me and my sister Mopsy. We lived with two young human females and they named us after two rabbits in a...gook? Dook? Oh, what's the word? Book, that's it! Whatever a book is. They let us hop all over the house and we used to watch the mother making food. Then the father said it wasn't clean, having rabbits in the kitchen. But I can tell you, we were at least as clean as they were! Anyway, we had to live in a tiny wooden house after that, and then the children got a kitten and we were let out less and less, so one day, when we got the chance, we escaped!"

"Oh, well done!" I said.

"See how brave an' clever rabbits are!" put in Robbo, swaggering around the room.

"And is Mopsy here as well?" I asked, and immediately wished I hadn't. I'd been too late to notice Isabel's warning look. Flopsy seemed to shrink into herself.

"I don't talk about that," she murmured, looking down at the leaves she was holding.

There was a brief awkward silence and Robbo sidled up and whispered in my ear, "She got eaten by a fox."

I felt a massive rush of guilt, as if I'd eaten Flopsy's sister myself. Oh why did foxes have to do that? If they'd only talk to rabbits, surely they wouldn't eat them.

"You must have had cheese, living with Harold and Edith," said Isabel, obviously trying to change the subject.

"Yeah," I said. "But I had no idea it was so complicated to make. Or that it was made from milk. And where do you get the milk from?"

Robbo rolled his eyes. "From cows, slug-brain!"

"So how do you get the cows to give you the milk?"

"Ah," said Robbo. "Tell you what, Fox-face – soon as you're better you can come on one of our little expeditions."

A few weeks later, I was fit enough to go outside the Hollow with Robbo. A group of rabbits was going to dig up vegetables from a nearby farm and I was allowed to go with them, as long as I didn't dig too hard and hurt my leg. It was a night-time operation, with Robbo giving orders like the leader of a gang of robbers.

"Right! When you're liberatin' vegetables, the most important thing is to cover your tracks. It's gotta look like there's no one bin here. So, number one group – top left corner, brussels sprouts. Just a few from each plant. Number two group – bottom right corner, carrots. Every fifth one, and don't forgit to pat the earth down afterwards.

"Yo, Fox-face, don't snigger!" he said. "Y'all be laughin' on the other side o' your face if the farmer found out and set traps for us."

"No, Robbo. Sorry."

I buried my nose in the earth I was digging, so he wouldn't see my grin.

Some of the animals were carrying sacks made of woven grasses, and when these were full, number one group dragged half back to the Hollow, while number two group hauled the other half to a low wooden building in another field.

Isabel dragged her sack over to me.

"You stay with me, Edgar," she whispered. "See that shed?"

I nodded.

"That's where the cows sleep in winter. It's easier when the weather gets warm and they stay out in the fields, but there's a way in. Follow me."

She led me to a hole in the side of the shed. It was big enough for a rabbit, but a bit of a squeeze for me. I managed to crawl through, though, and found myself in a warm, dark space filled by breathy noises and the odd gentle moo. Once my eyes had adjusted, I saw a row of gates on either side of a central aisle. There was plenty of space between the bottom of the gates and the ground, and Isabel and some other rabbits ducked underneath.

"Come on, Edgar," she called. "Come and meet Daffodil."

This was followed by a low moo.

Nervously, I stuck my head under the gate, and immediately backed away again. There was a monster lying down in there!

"Come on, Edgar! She's a friendly cow," called Isabel.

That was a cow? But it was enormous! I'd seen them at a distance but never realised they were so huge. This cow could have squashed Isabel to bits if it rolled on top of her.

"Oh, come on, don't be shy!"

Shy? Terrified more like. But I couldn't show Isabel. She'd think I was a real coward. So I crept under the gate and stayed as far from the cow as I could.

Isabel turned to it. Or should I say her?

"Here you are, Daffodil, I've brought you some nice vegetables. Makes a change from hay, doesn't it?"

Daffodil made a sort of grunting noise and buried her nose in the carrots and sprouts that Isabel tipped on to the ground.

"And now do you think I could have just a tiny drop of your milk?" the rabbit went on.

So Daffodil knelt up and Isabel pulled half a scooped-out pumpkin from the sack. I'd never seen pumpkins before I went to the Hollow but apparently the farmers grew them and the animals found them useful for all sorts of things. Now Isabel started squeezing a teat between her two forepaws and white stuff squirted into the pumpkin.

"Do you want a go?" she asked me, taking her paws off the cow's wobbly udder. I hastily shook my head.

"Er, p'raps next time," I mumbled. "I think it'd go all over the place if I tried it."

So this was how they got the milk to make the cheese. I was full of admiration. The Badgers' Hollow animals were clever!

Getting the pumpkin halves home without spilling all the milk seemed to be the hardest part. By the time they'd been pushed through the hole in the shed and carefully carried back to the cheese room, they were only about half full.

I was suddenly exhausted, and only too grateful to turn into the entrance to Harold and Edith's sett. The two old badgers were dozing by the oven.

"It's like a different world over here," I said to them, "and my family don't even know I'm safe. They don't know about you two or milking cows or anything. You haven't seen that owl, have you?"

"I have tried to find Benedict," yawned Harold. "I'm sure he'd be only too happy to fly over to Horn Wood with your news, but no one seems to know where he is. Come and warm yourself, Edgar. Don't worry, he'll turn up soon."

But I did worry. Yule was coming, and how could my family enjoy themselves if they didn't know I was safe? They had no idea about all the new exciting things I was discovering. For all they knew, I could be dead.

CHAPTER TWELVE

Yule

But then there was no time for worrying, because everyone was too busy getting ready for Yule. Edith was chopping wrinkly old apples for the mince patties, her daughter Emma was shelling walnuts for the nut roasts and Emma's four small cubs were rolling all over the floor throwing bits of shell at each other. I felt like joining in with them, but thought I'd better not. So I tried to help by fetching and carrying for Edith.

Like, "Fetch me the dried plums somebody."

Somebody meant me.

Or, "Somebody go and see what Harold's doing."

Again, *somebody* meant me.

And then one time when I was off to find Harold, he came in stamping his paws and fluffing up his fur to get warm and muttering something about a moot. Whatever that was.

"It's no good, you know, we'll have to have one," he said.

"One what, dear?" asked Edith, carrying on with her chopping.

"A moot. A moot. Weren't you listening?"

"Well, you were mumbling, dear," sighed Edith.

"What's a moot?" I asked, though I had a vague feeling Hugo had explained this to me.

"It's a...a moot is a..." Harold waved his forepaw vaguely around. "Didn't they have moots in Horn Wood?"

I shook my head.

Edith explained. "If there's something important to discuss, we all get together and...discuss it. That's what a moot is."

"Oh," I said, not all that much clearer. "So why do we need one now? What's happened?"

"Nothing's actually happened," said Harold, "or at least, not suddenly. It's been happening for quite a while, but so gradually that we didn't notice at first, did we?"

"No, dear," replied Edith," and I still think we don't need to worry about it before Yule. We've got enough to do at the moment, and moots can wait. I'm more interested in getting all these mince patties cooked."

"What *are* you talking about?" I asked again.

But then Harold said something that made me forget all about moots.

"I found that owl at last," he said. "Old Benedict Hootingly-ffeatherclaw. Apparently he's been away on a gliding holiday. He'll fly over to his cousin Aidan tonight and Aidan'll pass your news on to your family. All right, Edgar?"

"Oh, thank you! That's brilliant!"

That was the best news I could have had! I leapt up, itching to share it with somebody. But in this case *somebody* meant my best friend Cuthbert the badger.

"See you lot! I'm going in to Cuthbert's."

I scooted up the passageway with Edith's voice floating after me.

"Don't be long, and tell him we'll see him for supper as usual."

Once outside, I turned left, dived into the next opening, down another passage and into a room like the one I'd just left. But the scene inside could not have been more different.

Instead of the chatter and bustle next door, Cuthbert was sitting on the floor all alone beside three enormous earthenware jars. The fire at the base of the oven was mostly grey ash with just a few red embers still glowing. In the dim light of a small candle, I saw that Cuthbert was holding a little pot, out of which he scraped something golden and sticky-looking. He turned to me and the blissful expression on his face seemed to brighten the whole room. Then he stuck his paw in his mouth and sucked.

I had been going to say, 'Hey, Cuthbert, guess what!' but the words died on my lips. Instead I asked, "What are you doing?"

"Mm, I *love* honey," said Cuthbert. "Hello, Edgar. I'm making mead. It's 'cos I like parties so much, they've put me in charge of the drinks."

"How do you make mead?"

"Mostly honey and water, with a few other bits and pieces. But the honey's the most important bit."

Suck, suck.

"Is that for Yule?" I asked.

"Not this coming Yule. Don't you know anything? This lot won't be ready to drink for at least a couple of years. Don't they have mead where you come from?"

"Yeah, mead's one thing we did have, but I never learned how to make it."

I sniffed the jars with interest. So that was something else I'd have to learn. Then I looked around the room. It seemed gloomy and cavernous compared to next door, though it was about the same size. But Cuthbert looked as happy as ever.

"You're always so cheerful," I said. "Don't you get lonely, living here all on your own?"

"Me, lonely?" said Cuthbert. "I've got friends and relations all over the place. And I like to keep the old sett up."

"Your parents used to live here, didn't they?"

"Yes. I don't really remember them. I was only a baby when they died. Osbert brought me up, but he moved to another sett when he married Emma. The old place'd be lonely if I left as well. There's talk of some rabbits moving in, 'cos they're getting a bit crowded, but I'm not sure. It's always been a badger sett." Cuthbert's smile faded and he looked thoughtful. "D'you think I'm being selfish?"

"No," I said. "It's your home, after all… I know! Perhaps I could come and live with you!"

"You'd be very welcome, Edgar, but I think Edith likes looking after you."

Just then there came a scraping sound from the other side of the wall.

"What's that?" I said, startled.

"The rabbits next door, extending their burrow," said Cuthbert. "I told you, they're getting overcrowded."

"But I expect you'll be married one day and then you'll need a place big enough for a family, so you stay here." I paused. "Why aren't you married, Cuthbert? You're a bit older than me, aren't you?"

"Well," said Cuthbert, putting his head on one side, "it just hasn't happened yet. There aren't any badgers the right age in the Hollow. There was somebody nice in Brock Wood, but she didn't want to stop eating animals and I didn't want to move away from here…so…"

I sensed this was a delicate subject, but wasn't sure how to change it.

"There's plenty of time!" I said, a bit too brightly. "I haven't got a girlfriend yet either. Perhaps we'll end up making it a double wedding!"

Cuthbert didn't answer. He was having another suck.

"Anyway, come on, you greedy badger," I said. "Don't just sit there sucking your paws. I think it's time we put up some decorations."

Cuthbert's sticky mouth dropped open.

"That's what I've been saying to *you*, and you were never in the mood. What's happened?"

"I've had some good news! Benedict's back, and he's flying over to Aidan in Horn Wood for me! So now I'm in a holiday mood. Let's go and pick some mistletoe."

"That's wonderful, Edgar! I think that calls for a little drop of elderberry wine."

And the next day we started to decorate both the setts with holly, mistletoe and any other evergreens we could find.

"I love a party," said Cuthbert, as we hung ivy over the stones at the top of Edith's oven.

"Mind you don't set fire to the place!" she scolded. "I could do with a bit of help with all this cooking, as well."

Every home was filled with greenery and the smell of baking, and the badgers dragged an enormous fallen log into the dell at the centre of the Hollow. Edith had kept a piece of last year's Yule-log to light the new one.

"It's good luck, dear, and it's the proper way to do things. We might have changed some of our ways, but we still keep the old ways where it's important. The year turns, and we turn with it."

Just before the Festival, Aidan flew in with my longed-for

news. My family were well and they were overjoyed that I was safe and among friends! But these few words from home, that I'd been waiting so long to hear, somehow made me feel more unsettled. I told myself I was being stupid and tried hard to get back into the party mood.

I'd been too young to remember much about my first Longest Day, and I felt I'd been cheated out of the Autumn Offering, so I was doubly determined to enjoy my first Yule. Just like the others, I feasted on nut roast and mince patties and toasted everyone's health in mead. But when they all held paws and began to sing and dance around the log, I slipped into the shadows to watch.

Far above, frosty stars glittered in a black sky. The same sky that was arching over Horn Wood, on the other side of the death-strip. I felt it might as well have been on the other side of the world.

Cuthbert found me.

"Come on, Edgar," he said. "What's the matter?"

"Oh, nothing. I was just wondering what my family are doing now."

"Enjoying themselves, I expect, and that's what you should be doing too," said Cuthbert.

He grabbed my paw and whirled me into the dance around the blazing log.

CHAPTER THIRTEEN

The Moot

It took a while to get over all the partying.

"I never want to see another jar of mead," groaned Cuthbert.

"Serves you right," I said, though I wasn't feeling too good myself.

"Buck yourselves up!" said Harold. "We're arranging a moot!"

So on a frosty night in late midwinter, the first full moon after Yule, I found myself sitting on the edge of the Hollow dell where the Yule-log had been burnt. I gazed at the badgers across a crowd of wood mice, rabbits, field voles, squirrels, hedgehogs and moles. A huge round moon sailed over us all, shedding a light almost as bright as a winter's day. Next to me were the other foxes, as well as Robbo and Isabel. But I was more excited than anyone. My first moot! Then Cuthbert waddled up.

"Budge up," he said, and plonked himself down next to me.

"Why are we so honoured?" asked Isabel. "Aren't you gonna sit with the other badgers?"

"He'd rather sit with his mates, wouldn't you, Cuthbert?" Hugo grinned at him.

Cuthbert grinned back.

"Look at the fox in the moon," said Mildred dreamily, gazing up at the face in the great silver globe.

"The rabbit in the moon, you mean," said Isabel.

"We can all play that game," said Cuthbert. "I always thought it was a badger."

"Sh!" hushed Robbo. "It's starting."

As Harold stood up, raised his paw and cleared his throat, everyone stopped talking and looked at him.

"Thank you, friends, for coming here tonight," he began, "and a specially big thank you to those of you who'd normally be tucked up in bed."

The squirrels nodded sleepily.

"To start the proceedings, Robbo is going to entertain us with a...um...a *rap*."

Robbo stood up and swaggered to the front to cheers from the other young rabbits. Harold carried on with his introduction.

"I believe this is about...um...the advantages of...um... holding a moot. Is that correct?"

"Yep," said Robbo. "You said it!"

"I know I said it," growled Harold. "Oh...why don't you just begin."

And Robbo did.

"Yo, listen up folks and listen up good
An' I'll tell y'all a story about Horn Wood.
Now in Horn Wood lives a big ol' stag
An' what he does just ain't my bag.
He tell ya what to eat, he tell ya what to think,
He tell ya when to breathe, he tell ya when to blink.
An' if he don't like what you're about,
The next thing ya know he'll throw you out.

Yo, no one gits a say but him,
He'll throw y'all out on the slightest whim.
But the way we do things here in the Holler,
There's no one to lead and no one to foller.
Every animal gits their say,
That's the Badgers' Holler way.
So if doin' jus' what you're told don't suit,
Y'all should git together and have a MOOT!"

There was wild applause and cries of, "Yo, Robbo!" and, "Robbo's the king!" as he sauntered back to his place. But *I* was thrilled. That was *my* story the rap was telling!

"Thank you so much, Robert – I mean, *Robbo*," Harold corrected himself as Robbo swung indignantly round. "And now I'm going to call on my good wife to say a few words, before we begin to discuss our problem."

"What problem?" muttered a rabbit.

Harold sat down again on the frozen ground, and Edith rose.

"I shan't keep you long, my dears," she began.

"That's a relief," yawned a wood mouse.

"But I simply wanted to remind you of something. When we first founded this community there was some trouble from local stoats and weasels. We were forced to defend the smaller animals, and our good friend Hubert Herbwise, father of Osbert and Cuthbert, lost his life in that fight. And that is how valuable our way of life is to us. So precious that we are prepared to die for it."

She paused, and everyone looked serious. I was fascinated. I'd no idea that the Hollow had such violent beginnings.

"Since then we've managed to live in harmony with our neighbours, especially our good friends in Brock Wood. And we were delighted to be joined by some foxes, first Hugo, then Mildred, and now Edgar."

Everyone turned to stare at us, and we shuffled uncomfortably and looked at the ground embarrassed.

"I'm nearly finished, my dears," Edith went on. "What I haven't mentioned yet is the number of other animals who live here happily with us – all you mice, rabbits, squirrels and so on. We do love having you here, but there is a problem, which I'm going to ask my husband to explain."

"At last," whispered Robbo. "Takin' their time gittin' to the point, ain't they?"

Harold stood up again and looked around gravely at everyone.

"Friends," he said, "there are just too many of us! We're starting to get overcrowded. You've all benefited from our peaceful ways and gone about your business without fear of being eaten, but if we don't do something soon, a new danger will await us – starvation!"

Everyone gasped and then started talking at once.

"It's true, you know," said an old wood mouse. "Half my family had to leave last summer, because there wasn't enough food for us all. It's better than your children being eaten, though."

"It's the same with us," said a mother rabbit, with six young rabbits sleepily lolling against her. "Three of my brothers left the warren last year to find new homes, and we're always having to go outside the Hollow to find enough food."

"Quiet please," called Harold, raising a paw. "One at a time, or we'll never reach a decision."

A grandfather rabbit stood up to speak.

"It's obvious really," he said. "Some of us have been thinking this for a while. If we're not being picked off and eaten by bigger animals, then we'll have to have smaller families."

"How can we do that?" piped up a mother vole. "I can't decide to have two babies instead of six. It just happens."

"Of course you can't," answered the rabbit. "But you can stick to one lot of babies. Have one family and no more."

"But they do get picked off," objected a mouse. "My Oliver was caught by a hawk before Yule."

His wife burst into tears, and he hugged her.

"That's a good point," said the vole. "Us mammals all live peaceably enough, but the birds have never stopped hunting around here...except for Aidan and Benedict."

Edith stood up.

"That's very true," she nodded. "It was kind of Aidan and Benedict to stop hunting in the Hollow, but if we didn't lose the odd neighbour to a hawk or kestrel, we'd be even more overcrowded. I think we should get back to what our friend Henry was saying. There was a lot of sense in it."

The grandfather rabbit stood up again and bowed, and Robbo whispered, "See – it takes a rabbit to talk sense."

Harold hushed everyone.

"We held this moot because we wanted people to decide for themselves. We've been thinking this for a while, us badgers, that if only people wouldn't have so many children, it might just solve the problem. Only *might*, mind you. We'll have to try it and see. So discuss it among yourselves for a few minutes, and then we'll have a vote."

I thought back to what Mum had said: "If we didn't eat some of them, the whole wood would be overrun with rabbits." It seemed she'd had a point.

For about two minutes, the dell was buzzing with conversation and argument, until a black shape glided across the moon. I looked up and saw the outline of an owl swooping towards us.

There was a few seconds' panic, with parents clutching their shrieking children, then a sigh of relief, when Aidan landed beside the badgers.

"A moooot, I see, and a good thing toooo," he hooted, "but a council of war's the thing for yoooo."

"What do you mean?" demanded Harold.

"It's not good nyoooos, oh, what a to-doooo." He kept bobbing his head up and down excitedly. "A raiding party – it groooo and groooo – from Horn Wood, and coming this way, toooo. Foxes, badgers, stoats and weasels – quite a fyoooo. I floooo overhead and got a good vyoooo. They haven't reached the tunnel, it's troooo, but it won't be long before they're throooo."

What?

No! From Horn Wood? I couldn't believe it!

There was a stunned silence, then Edith blurted out, "But why, why?"

"I don't know why, it came out of the bloooo, but I could make a guess or twoooo. Food's always scarce in the winter – too troooo – and someone's spread roooomours of rich pickings here among yoooo. Oh, what a to-doooo, what a to-doooo. You're in a styoooo."

Edith lowered her head and put her paws over her nose. Then she looked up, first at Harold, then around at the rest of us. Everyone seemed to be waiting for the badgers to come up with an answer.

"Oh, what's to be done?" she asked miserably.

"Don't ask me, I haven't a cloooo. But I'd think pretty quick, if I were yoooo!"

CHAPTER FOURTEEN

Battle Plans

I sat stunned in the rumpus that followed. Children wailed, parents tried to hush them and everybody was talking at once.

What was I going to do? Animals I knew must be heading this way. Not my family, surely. They knew I was here. But how could I fight animals I'd grown up with?

But then, how could I desert my friends in the Hollow?

At least I wouldn't be singled out as somebody's dinner. No one wanted to eat foxes. A lot of comfort that'd be, though, if I died defending the others.

"Edgar! Edgar! Have you gone deaf?" Hugo shouted in my ear.

"Sorry. I was miles away."

"Yeah, we noticed," said Hugo. "Listen! Mildred reckons we've got to get down to the death-strip tunnel. If we can fight them off one by one as they try to come through, we should manage okay even if there *are* a lot of them. We're just going to tell Harold and Edith and then we're off." He paused. "But what about you? You're in a funny position, aren't you?"

I nodded. "I can't seem to think straight."

Just then, Harold called for quiet.

"Please, friends, try not to panic," he began. "Before we do anything else, I need some volunteers to run to the tunnel. That's our first and most important line of defence."

"Us!" called Hugo and Mildred together.

"And us!" shouted two sturdy young badgers.

"Good!" said Harold. "When you get there, see if you can find anything to block it off a bit – some rocks, or maybe uproot a bush. Anything to make it harder for them to get through."

"That's a good idea," muttered Mildred.

"We need someone with a bit of experience," continued Harold. "Algie, perhaps you could go with them and organise things."

"Only too glad," growled Algie, who looked as if he could block up the tunnel all by himself.

"Off you go then," said Harold. "We'll send you word of any further plans... And good luck!" he called after them, as Hugo and Mildred streaked off, with the badgers lumbering along behind.

"Now, the next thing is to send to our friends in Brock Wood. Some of them may be willing to help us, though it's a lot to ask, and we mustn't *expect* them to come. Aidan, we wondered if you could fly there for us."

"Glad to get out of this hullabaloooo. I'll go straight away, if it's all right with yoooo."

And he took to the air. His great wings flapped a few times and then carried him silently in the direction of Brock Wood.

Edith spoke next.

"Listen, my dears," she began. "There's lots of you – most of you in fact – who won't be much good in a fight."

"I can fight!" declared Robbo. "Bring 'em on!"

"Fighting rabbits is one thing, Robbo, but we're talking about foxes, weasels, stoats and badgers. You won't have much chance against their sharp teeth and claws."

Robbo looked crestfallen, but for once he didn't argue.

"But what you rabbits are brilliant at is digging," Edith went on. "We want absolutely everybody, apart from badgers and foxes, to take shelter in the rabbit burrows and badger setts."

"So what d'you want us rabbits to do?" asked Robbo impatiently.

"Yes, yes, I was coming to that. When everyone's inside, with all the winter stores and as much water as we can carry in quickly, we want you rabbits to block up the entrances. Try and make it look as if there isn't an entrance there, if you can, though that'll be difficult. Then we want you to dig some little air holes, but try and make them so no one would notice them. Or perhaps you'd better dig the air holes first."

"Never mind what order they do it in, just get a move on!" said Harold. "And you'll have to make the burrows and setts a bit bigger. I told you – we're getting overcrowded. Now move!"

It didn't take long for all the families of small animals to be ready to go underground, with the food and water. It seemed that even Emma was going down below with her cubs, though she didn't look very happy about leaving Osbert.

And I sat stupidly watching and listening. I knew I should be doing something but I couldn't seem to move. Why didn't they give me a job? I had a horrible feeling that people were avoiding me. Did they wonder which side I was on? That thought almost gave me the energy to get up. Almost, but not quite.

Robbo, of course, ran around giving orders. He was directing a team of rabbits who were working underground. Earth was flying out of entrance holes everywhere.

"Hang on, what are you doing? That's a lot of earth. I only said make the burrows a *bit* bigger," said Harold. "Stop, everyone!"

"Stop, everyone!" went the order into various tunnels. Lots of rabbit heads appeared and looked at Robbo and Harold.

"We're joinin' up all the burrows and setts to make one great big warren," said Robbo. "That'll make more escape routes if any raiders get in."

"Well, thank you for telling us," said Harold.

"No time to waste on words!" said Robbo.

"I'm not sure if that's a good idea," put in Osbert. "If a weasel did get in, it'd have a free run everywhere."

"But no one'd be trapped!" said Robbo. "That's the point!"

"It's as broad as it's long, really," muttered Harold. "Okay, General. Carry on."

Robbo looked down his nose at Osbert, who was grumbling under his breath, and told the rabbits to keep working. They dived back down and were very soon joined by some of the smaller animals.

There were mice scampering up tunnels dragging nutshells of soil behind them. There were teams of voles dragging small pumpkin-halves of soil, and there were squirrels and young rabbits who could manage to push a half-pumpkin on their own. Once the soil was outside it was quickly spread around.

Finally, all the small animals vanished down below and all the front entrances except one were carefully disguised with grass and evergreens. Only when that was done did every rabbit disappear into the final entrance, under a blackthorn bush, and block it up from the inside.

Suddenly the moonlit dell was almost empty. I still sat there, feeling as if I was stuck to the ground. Then Cuthbert came and sat by me. He smiled sympathetically but didn't say anything.

The other badgers looked solemnly round at each other.

"Well, it's up to us now. Feels a bit lonely, doesn't it?" said Harold.

No one replied. Then Edith spoke.

"Don't you think a few more of us should make for the tunnel? We mustn't leave the Hollow completely deserted, but that's where the action's going to be."

"Good idea," said Harold, and four more of them, including Osbert and Cuthbert, set off for the death-strip.

"But remember, Osbert," said Edith, "only fight if you really have to. You're more use as a healer."

"See you later, Edgar," called Cuthbert breezily, as if he was going to a party, not a fight.

That left Harold, Edith and two other old badgers sitting with me in the central dell, where not that long ago the Yule celebrations had been held.

A cloud passed over the moon, and in the darkness we heard a barking noise and the sound of fighting.

"That sounds close," said Edith.

I suddenly came to life.

"I know that bark," I gasped, and sped off in the direction of the tunnel.

In no time at all I saw the four badgers surrounding a vixen. Her ears were flat, her teeth were bared and a menacing growl was coming from her throat. But she'd have no chance against the four of them, however brave she was.

"Stop! Stop!" I shouted. "Don't hurt her! That's my sister!"

CHAPTER FIFTEEN

Attack!

The badgers backed off and Elfreda and I smothered each other with licks and nuzzles.

"It's all right, it's all right, I haven't come to fight," panted Elfreda.

"Oh dear," said Osbert. "We do apologise. I hope we didn't hurt you. What must you think of us?"

"We're not usually like this," said Cuthbert. "Normally we're quite friendly, aren't we, Edgar."

I laughed, then started chasing Elfreda round in a circle.

"Meet my friends!" I yelled. "Friends, meet my sister, Elfreda!"

"Stop it!" said Elfreda, though she was laughing too. "Stop it, Edgar, you've gone barmy!"

"Yes, calm down, Edgar," chuckled Osbert. "We've got to get on to the tunnel. If you're sure you're all right, Elfreda?"

"I'm fine," panted Elfreda, "but I'm not sure about him!"

"Okay, go on," I said. "I'm a perfectly sensible, serious fox, and I definitely think you should get down to the tunnel."

So for the second time, the badgers said goodbye and went

lumbering on their way.

"I've been running as fast as I could," said Elfreda. "I wanted to warn you. I didn't think you'd already know."

I nodded, and at last my smile started to fade. "Aidan told us. But how many are coming?"

"Lots! Not our family, of course, except..." she trailed off.

"Except what?" I asked.

"Except I'm not sure about Ethel. I left her arguing with Mum and Dad."

"Trust Ethel," I sighed. "But how did you get past our sentries at the tunnel?"

"I just explained who I was, but *these* badgers weren't in a listening mood. Anyway, this is no time for chatting – or party games. You've got to get out of here double quick!"

"Why?"

"Well, obviously, it's dangerous round here," said Elfreda. "You don't want to get killed!"

Suddenly everything became clear for me. I felt as if I was waking up from a dream. How could I have doubted?

"No!" I burst out. "These are my friends – I can't desert them! They saved my life and they've given me a home. And they think like me, Elfreda. I'm not the odd one out here."

Elfreda put her head on one side and looked hard at me.

"But Edgar," she said, "there are a lot of old friends coming, and even our cousins, the Bushytails. How can you fight people you grew up with?"

"What did they do for me when the Great Stag sent me away? Did anyone stick up for me then? The Badgers' Hollow animals are my *real* friends."

"There wasn't much they *could* do. It's hard to go against the Great Stag," said Elfreda.

"I know," I admitted. "I'd like to give him a piece of my mind."

"It was giving him a piece of your mind that got you sent away in the first place!"

There was a sudden hubbub from the direction of the tunnel.

"It's started!" I gasped. "I've got to go, and I haven't even asked how Mum and Dad are."

"Oh, they're all right, but they wouldn't be if they knew you were going to be fighting."

"Look, Elfreda, I've got to. Why don't you go to Brock Wood and look up the Keenears family. This isn't your fight after all."

Elfreda looked back towards the tunnel, and then at Edgar.

"Okay, but I feel like a coward. I wish you'd come with me."

"Sorry," said Edgar, shaking his head. "We'll meet up again when it's over. I'll be fine, you'll see."

Another quick nuzzle and we raced off in different directions.

When I arrived, I found that Hugo, Mildred and the badgers had blocked the bottom half of the tunnel entrance with earth. It looked as if it would be easy to dig through – there had been no time to pack it tightly. But the stripy face poking over the top was clearly surprised to find it there.

"What's going on?" it growled.

"This is not your territory," snarled Algie. "Go back to Horn Wood."

The face turned around, and they heard a mumbled conversation. Then it turned back to them.

"We have no quarrel with you," said the stripy face, "but we're hungry. We've heard there's plenty of meat to spare over here. Enough for you and us as well."

"Who told you?" demanded Mildred.

"Our leader, the Great Stag," came the reply.

"Thought so," snorted Osbert. "Well, he's got no business sending you into our territory."

"But it's been a hard winter," said the badger.

"That's no excuse," said Cuthbert.

Two powerful sharp-clawed paws appeared on top of the earth bank as the badger tried to heave himself over it. Then, "Hey!" he shouted, as he ploughed into it, pushed from behind. The middle of the earth bank collapsed under his weight and he scrabbled round trying to regain his balance.

"If only we'd had time to do a better job," muttered Hugo, as the animals from the Hollow closed in on the tunnel entrance.

I had no doubts now. I didn't recognise this badger, but even if I had, how dare he come raiding into our territory!

Before the invader could right himself, Hugo grabbed him by the scruff of the neck and tried to shove him back into the tunnel. The badger bellowed, then twisted himself round and gave Hugo a sharp nip on the nose. Hugo yelped and let go, but Algie's full weight fell on the newcomer and pinned him down. Mildred bared her teeth at the next one who appeared in the tunnel mouth.

"We won't hurt him if you go back," she growled.

"Oh, won't we?" muttered Algie.

The second badger lunged at Mildred, but I flew at him and we all managed to bundle both the Horn Wood badgers back into the tunnel. There wasn't much left of the earth bank by now, but there was a solid wall of animals ready to attack anyone who tried to get through.

So far things were going as planned. But then…

Suddenly the fierce, pointed face of a large stoat thrust itself to the tunnel entrance. It shot out, straight at my throat! I ducked my head, and the stoat's teeth gripped the back of my neck.

A burning pain shot through me and I tried to shake the creature off, but before I knew what was happening, it screamed and let go. Cuthbert was sinking his teeth into its back.

The stoat twisted its snaky body round and tried to attack Cuthbert's face, but the badger's strong jaws tightened until it squealed, and then drooped lifeless. Cuthbert flung the body away.

Behind that stoat, though, had been a weasel, and then another stoat, and then there were stoats, weasels, badgers and foxes everywhere. The line of defence was broken!

All at once the air was filled with snarls and ripping claws and jagged fangs. The rank smells of stoat and weasel mingled with the fox and badger scents that I knew so well. I had no time to worry whether I recognised anyone. They weren't individuals – just one seething mass.

I could taste warm blood...my own, or someone else's?

"Here!" yelled Algie, from the left of the tunnel. "Don't let them get through!"

I sprang to his side and headed off a young stoat who was sneaking round the side of the fighting. "Grrr!" bubbled up from the back of my throat as I crouched in my most menacing posture. The stoat bared its teeth but I lunged and knocked it off balance. We rolled over and over, each trying to find a spot to sink teeth into. I got there first. I twisted my head and managed to grab a mouthful of the stoat's white underbelly. The stoat shrieked and tore itself away, then scooted back towards the tunnel.

But just as I was thinking, well that was easy, snapping jaws shot at me out of nowhere and I found myself grappling with a weasel. I tried to get a grip on it, anywhere, but its wriggling body seemed impossible to pin down… I was *much* bigger than the weasel – surely I could beat it! But that was the problem. There was nothing to get hold of. It was all fluid muscle, like a thick furry snake.

Then its thorn-sharp teeth found my ear. I heard an anguished yowl and realised that it was coming from my own throat. My ear was on fire!… Desperately, I shook my head. I wouldn't have any ear left!

A massive shape loomed up in front of me. I braced myself. A stripy snout thrust itself at me, fangs bared…but…what was happening?

The badger reared up with a fox at its throat – was it Hugo? They swayed for a few seconds as if in some ghastly dance. Then the badger gave a strangled, gurgling cry and blood gushed from its neck. It fell, like a mountain, on top of me. I tried to crawl away as it thrashed about but when it finally slumped into death, I was still underneath.

The weasel was thrown off, and I tried to draw breath. But I couldn't. I couldn't move, couldn't even see as the crushing weight pressed down on my head and upper body. The last breath was squeezed from my lungs, and then… I was no longer there.

CHAPTER SIXTEEN

The Voice

I found myself floating in some dark place above the battle, dimly aware of the commotion below. Well – it was nothing to do with me now. They'd have to fight without me.

I could hear my own voice, saying to Elfreda: "We'll meet up when it's over. I'll be fine, you'll see." You didn't always get things right.

I felt strangely peaceful, though. I knew that I was facing death but somehow, floating in the dark, I didn't seem to mind. Looking down at the battleground I watched the knots of fighting. Was that Algie or one of the Horn Wooders? It was hard to see who was who. It would all work out in the end, I thought calmly.

Then I noticed, in a detached sort of way, some animal streaking across to my body. I could tell it was mine by the one white paw sticking out from underneath the badger. The animal – it was a fox – stuck its nose and front paws under the badger and slowly rolled it off. Then it pushed my mouth open and started to blow.

There was a whooshing sensation. All at once I was back in my body, and it hurt!

The voice of a young vixen hissed in my ear, "Get out of here, you fool. This isn't your fight."

That wasn't right, I thought vaguely. That was what I'd said to Elfreda: "This isn't your fight."

The vixen nosed me up on to my legs and shoved me away from the tunnel.

"Move, you idiot," she hissed again.

It was Ethel.

But before I had time even to think what to say to her, a great voice boomed out from the other side of the death-strip.

"Stop! Stop this fighting immediately!"

Everyone froze. The voice was used to being obeyed, and it didn't occur to anyone to disobey it. I looked up and saw, clearly outlined against the starry sky, the owner of the voice. The black shape of the Great Stag, antlers held high, seemed to tower over everything.

I could barely stand, but I looked at my sister's face, then back again at the Stag, and something boiled up inside me. I stumbled across to the tunnel and somehow dragged myself through it and out the other side. No one was moving apart from me.

The Great Stag stood like a rock, but I didn't stop until I reached him. A green mist was floating in front of my eyes… I lowered my head until it cleared away and then looked up. The Stag seemed to have turned to stone.

Ignoring the pain in my chest, I gasped enough air into my lungs to let out a frenzied howl.

"You!" I yelled. "This is all your fault! You love killing, don't you, but you get other animals to do it for you! You haven't got the guts to do it yourself!"

The Stag gazed down at me, and I stared up in astonishment. Where was that scornful curl of the lip that I remembered? For the Stag's eyes were like two deep wells filled with sadness.

Time seemed to stop.

Then at last the Stag spoke. Although he called me by my family name, he spoke as if he was talking to everyone.

"That is not true, Sharpeyes," he began. "I do not kill, because it is not in a deer's nature to kill other creatures. I do not love killing, but I do love nature and her ancient ways.

"I am a king and my people were hungry. Winter is always hard. I told them what I knew, that there was food over here.

"This was meant to be a hunting raid, not a battle. I did not think the territory would be so fiercely defended. I did not mean animals to die fighting each other. The hunted, yes. They are prey to the hunter. That is nature's way. But not this kind of bloodshed."

The Stag bowed his head and was silent for a moment. Then he raised it again and his voice rang out.

"I wish the fighting to stop and all the wounded to be cared for. We relinquish any claim to food outside our own land."

I gazed up at the noble head, then, half ashamed but still half defiant, I couldn't resist saying, "You were wrong then. Do you admit you were wrong?"

I heard a gasp from the surrounding animals. The Stag's expression changed for an instant – his eyes widened and his nostrils flared. I shrank back, but the face softened again.

"Sharpeyes," said the Stag, now clearly talking only to me, "I may not have made the right decision on every occasion in my life. But I have many responsibilities. If you reach my age without ever making a mistake, I shall be very surprised."

I hung my head and didn't answer.

"Where is the leader of your community?" the Stag continued.

"We haven't exactly got one," I mumbled. "Harold and Edith,

I suppose you mean. They're back at the Hollow."

"Ask them if they would be so good as to meet me here three nights from now. That should give everyone time to recover. It will soon be light and we must all withdraw."

"I will," I said, and backed away into the tunnel. I was sure I was going to be sick.

Just then there was a rumpus on my side of the death-strip, as reinforcements arrived from Brock Wood.

"Where's the fight, then?" growled a burly-looking badger when I staggered out of the tunnel. He seemed disappointed to hear that it was over, but lots of the other animals looked relieved. Everyone who was unhurt turned to and started to take care of the wounded. I stared dazedly around and then collapsed.

The Brock Wood healers, a vixen and a dog-fox, were busying themselves cleaning and dressing wounds and putting sprained limbs into splints. The vixen came up to me and pulled a leather flagon out of her bag.

"Lift your head," she said, kindly but briskly. "I saw you walk just now, so I don't think anything's broken."

I weakly shook my head. Then she pulled out the stopper and held the flagon to my mouth. Fire-water! I coughed and spluttered as my throat burned. But gradually, as I got my breath back, a warm glow spread through my insides.

"What is it?" he gasped.

"My magic potion," grinned the vixen. "Family secret. It doesn't bring the dead back to life, but that's about all it doesn't do."

I managed a feeble smile. "Go on," I said. "I'll be all right. There's others need you more than me."

"Take care, then," said the vixen, and moved on to her next patient.

I looked around. Where was Osbert? It wasn't like him to leave this sort of thing to somebody else. I gingerly tried my legs and found that I could stand.

Oh, there was Osbert. I tottered towards him. He was crouching over something. Over...what? No...it couldn't be... No, surely... But it was. Osbert was bowed in grief, his face buried in his brother's neck.

Cuthbert was dead.

CHAPTER SEVENTEEN

Going Home

Osbert's body shook with sobs as I sank numbly down beside him. The sobs gradually died down and he lifted his head to look at me.

"First Father, then Mother, now Cuthbert," he choked out, before collapsing again with a wail of despair.

I nosed him gently. My mind didn't seem to be working. There was nothing to say anyway, so I pressed my body against Osbert's heaving side and stroked him with the side of my head. I don't know how long we stayed like that.

"Come on, Edgar," Elfreda's voice murmured in my ear. "I came back to help, but there's plenty of others here."

"Yes, come on," said Ethel. "They want to carry him home."

Slowly and shakily Osbert and I stood up. Four badgers gently lifted Cuthbert's body on to a stretcher and started to carry him on his last journey back to the Hollow.

It was that quiet time before dawn and Osbert, now silent, padded beside the stretcher in the grey light. The Horn Wood dead were being carried away and the wounded from both sides limped or were carried back to their homes. I stood and looked on as if in a trance.

Cuthbert couldn't be dead...he couldn't be! He was too cheerful, too...alive! He enjoyed things too much – honey, dancing, having a laugh with his friends... And who'd look after all that mead he'd brewed?... What a stupid thing to think! Fancy thinking about mead, when Cuthbert was dead!

By now, I couldn't see anything but a blur. I brushed the tears away, but it was no good. More kept coming.

"It's not fair," I burst out as we watched Osbert walk, head bowed, beside Cuthbert's body. "His father died in the Battle of the Hollow, and now his brother's been killed. It's just not fair, both from the same family."

Ethel looked at me.

"Life isn't fair," she said, "and there's nothing you can do about it, with all your high ideals."

I had nothing to say to that. It seemed Ethel was right. But then wasn't it worth trying to make it a bit fairer? I couldn't think about that now. Instead I bowed my head and once again my eyes started to fill with tears.

"He was my best friend," I mumbled.

Elfreda rubbed her head against my side.

"Why don't you come back with us, Edgar," she said, "and see Mum and Dad. You could meet them outside the wood, if you don't want to disobey the Stag."

"Yes...yes, I will," I said, "but come to the Hollow first. I must make sure my friends are all right. Only...only you must behave yourself, Ethel."

Ethel grinned and nodded, and we trotted slowly back to Badgers' Hollow, tired, thirsty, and in my case limping from a torn paw. Just before we got there, I was violently sick.

But when we arrived, there was more bad news!

Harold was lying in the dell, bleeding heavily from a deep

gash in the side of his neck. Osbert had pulled himself together and was carefully cleaning the wound, while Edith held Harold's paw.

I didn't want to disturb them, so I looked around for someone else to ask. Then I saw Hugo and Mildred.

"What's happened?"

"You could ask those heroes," spat Mildred, "if they were alive."

She pointed to a little heap of weasel bodies.

"Lucky some Brock Wooders came here, as well as to the tunnel," said Hugo. "This lot managed to slip through without being noticed. Hoping to have a nice little feast of mice and rabbits all to themselves, they were. Harold and Edith are brave, but they're getting on a bit, and so are the other two. The Brock Wooders got here just in time."

I looked at the weasels. Now they were dead they looked tiny, but I remembered what savage fighters they'd been in the battle. My torn ear was still hurting.

"You wouldn't think such small creatures could do such a lot of damage, would you?" I said.

"Well, there were seven of them, and they're vicious little blighters," said Hugo.

"We'll bury them outside the Hollow," added Mildred.

I limped over to Harold.

"How is he?" I whispered to Edith, but she didn't answer.

Then Emma bustled across, carrying a cold compress of herbs from Osbert's stores. One of her children trotted behind her.

"What's wrong with Granddad?" he piped up.

Emma shushed him and hustled him back to their sett.

"Now try and keep still while I tie this on, Harold," said Osbert. "It should help to stop the bleeding."

Harold winced as Osbert gently put on the compress, and bound it with strands of wool.

"Is it still dark, Edith?" he groaned.

"Well, it's starting to get light, dear," Edith replied, stroking his paw.

"I can't see properly, Osbert. Everything looks dim and there are things floating round in front of my eyes."

Osbert sat back and shook his head. "I think you're getting a bit of a fever. What you need is a good rest. You'll feel better in the morning."

The entrances to the setts and burrows were being unblocked, and Harold was carefully carried into his own sett on a stretcher.

I sank to the ground. What else could go wrong? I watched grey hind quarters disappear into Harold and Edith's entrance tunnel and then felt my eyes drawn to another entrance, just to the right. Like the others it had been hastily unblocked, and small animals stood round it in mournful groups. Some were rubbing their eyes.

Cuthbert's sett. My eyes filled with tears again and I turned away, trying to blank it out of my mind.

"Come back with us. You need a change of scenery," said Ethel. "Besides, I'm not sure how much longer I can stay here, with all these juicy young rabbits around."

Through all my grief, I couldn't help smiling.

"But perhaps you're not feeling well enough," said Elfreda anxiously.

"That was some weight you were squashed under," said Ethel. "I thought you'd have a few broken ribs."

"No, I'm sore," I sniffed, "but I feel a lot better now I've been sick. I don't know what was in that drink the vixen gave me, but whatever it was, it worked."

"Your ear looks a bit chewed," said Elfreda.

"That's because it was," said Edgar. "Look, I will come with you – I really want to see Mum and Dad – but I must just pass a message on to this…juicy young rabbit."

I beckoned Robbo over.

"Listen, Robbo. The Great Stag wants a meeting with Harold and Edith in three nights' time. On the other side of the tunnel. Can you tell them? I'm off to see my family, but I'll be back very soon. Look after everyone, won't you… Osbert and Harold and everyone."

"Sure thing," said Robbo. "I always do."

I turned my back on it all and we three foxes slipped through woods and along hedgerows, under the death-strip and all the way back to Horn Wood.

I felt torn in two. Was it right to leave the Hollow now, when they might need me? Harold would be all right, wouldn't he? He'd got Edith and Osbert to look after him. And Emma, of course. She'd look after her father. And Osbert would be all right, wouldn't he? Emma would look after him as well, and his children would cheer him up. Emma was going to be busy. Well, there were other animals. And Robbo would boss everyone around. And I wouldn't be gone long.

And then I finally began to realise that I was going to see Mum and Dad again. That was why I was going. Never mind that old Stag. I was going to see my mum and dad and I was going into the wood. I was going home!

Tired as we were, we reached Horn Wood far more quickly than I expected. My old home was much nearer than I'd thought! When I'd first left it, several moons ago, it had seemed as if I were setting out for the other side of the world. I was younger then and

I'd hardly been outside the wood. I was in shock, too, about being thrown out and having to leave everyone I loved.

But now we all knew where we were going. There were no instructions about having a good sleep before we tried to cross the death-strip. We just plodded steadily on.

And there it was, waiting for me! Horn Wood! But it had changed. Then, it had glowed with autumn reds and golds. Now the trees stood bare, their branches black and lacy against the dawn sky.

As we got nearer, Ethel slipped on ahead, and just before I reached the first trees two pointed faces peered out at us. I couldn't believe it. I'd dreamed of this and here they were.

Mum and Dad.

They looked astonished. Then Ethel bounded out with a big grin on her face. I stood still for a few heartbeats and then we all rushed at each other and rolled over and over, Ethel, Elfreda, Mum, Dad and me.

The pale wintry sun rose over the treetops and we all licked and nuzzled and laughed and nosed and rubbed each other and licked again.

I was home.

CHAPTER EIGHTEEN

Snow

At last Mum said, "Snoozing snails, Edgar, you can hardly keep your eyes open. I don't care about the Great Stag – you come and have a good sleep in your own home. I'd like a look at those cuts and grazes too. Your poor ear!"

So I found myself back in our earth, my wounds bathed, curled up with Ethel and Elfreda. We slept the rest of the day away, and woke up with enticing food smells tickling our nostrils.

I yawned, stretched, winced slightly with a pain in my ribs and then realised that I felt very hungry.

"Mm, breakfast," said Ethel, licking her lips. "I smell fried water vole. Dad's been down to the river."

"What about you, Edgar?" asked Elfreda, rubbing her eyes. "You won't eat that, will you?"

"No, and I'm famished," I said. "I wonder what else is in the larder."

Mum came bustling in, all smiles.

"How's your paw, my love?" she asked.

I looked at my paw in surprise.

"It feels fine," I said. "I forgot I'd even hurt it." I stretched myself again and flexed my legs. "I'm a bit achy and my ear stings, but most of all – I'm hungry!"

Mum laughed. "What can I get you? I'm afraid it's the wrong time of year for eggs or blackberries, but there are still some mushrooms in the larder."

"Mushrooms would be great," I said. "I'm afraid I don't eat worms any more."

"Hiccupping hedgehogs!" exploded Ethel. "Don't tell me worms are clan-folk!"

"Shut up, Ethel!" giggled Elfreda.

"All right, I know it sounds weird," I said, "but I've found out it's possible to live without killing anything, and that's what I'm trying to do."

I left Ethel with her mouth hanging open and followed Mum into the living room, where I buried my face in a bowlful of mushrooms she'd already fried for me.

"I thought you were all starving over here, from what the Great Stag said," I mumbled.

"Don't talk with your mouth full, Edgar," said Mum, though she didn't sound as if she minded.

When the bowls were washed and put away, Dad cleared his throat. "Now, son, delighted as we are to see you, we do realise that you'll be off again soon, back to that Badgers' Hollow. I can't tell you how amazed we were to hear that you'd found a whole bunch of animals who lived like you wanted to. Surely the Great Stag must have realised you'd run into them. Perhaps he thought you'd just stay there and not infect anyone over here with your funny ideas."

I laughed.

"I'd love you all to meet them," I said, "specially Harold and Edith. And there's Osbert." His face darkened. "Poor Osbert. His brother was killed last night... Cuthbert... He was my best friend. And Harold was attacked by weasels and..." Suddenly I felt guilty about enjoying myself so much. "Yes, I ought to go back soon. But the thing is, now I know how close we are, I can pop over about once a week. I must have been stupid not to see how easy it'd be."

"You were too much in awe of the Great Stag," put in Mum. "We all were. I can't believe we didn't kick up a bit more fuss when he threw you out. Still, it seems to have worked out all right for you."

"It would have worked out even better if you'd known about the death-strip tunnel," I grinned.

"Oh, don't," shuddered Mum. "I can't bear to think of it!"

She put a paw over one of mine, and then Dad went on.

"The thing is, son, we're going on a family hunting expedition tonight, us and the Bushytails, and we wondered if you wanted to come along, just for old time's sake. You needn't kill anything – you could just be the lookout."

"Well... I'm not sure," I said.

I didn't want to offend anyone, and an outing would be fun. It did seem ridiculous, though, to risk my life one night to stop small animals being killed and then the next night to go on a hunt.

"It's only chickens," put in Ethel slyly, "but I suppose chickens are clan-folk now, as well?"

"Well, I don't know about clan-folk, but the thing is, they are creatures with feelings, like us."

Ethel rolled her eyes, shook her head and sighed.

"Look, you two," said Dad, "that's enough of that. We all know how Edgar thinks, Ethel, and even if we disagree with him, there's no need to make a song and dance about it.

"The point is, son, there's a new chicken farm been built,

with *no* dogs. It's an odd sort of place, just loads of great big barns. You never see the chickens pecking about outside, and for a long time we thought they were just for storing grain and suchlike. But your Uncle Rufus has definitely seen chickens being taken in, and Elfreda's seen boxes of eggs being taken out."

"They dropped one and all the eggs smashed. That's how I know," said Elfreda.

"So it seems worth investigating. Won't you come, Edgar, just to keep watch for us? It'd be great to go out as a family once more."

I looked at their pleading faces and decided. It *would* be fun to run with my family under a starry sky and sniff the old scents of my home territory.

"All right, I'll come, but I won't have anything to do with any killing."

"Great!" said Elfreda, and Ethel grinned at me.

"Now that's settled, go and look outside," said Mum. "There's something you three haven't seen before."

We dashed up the tunnel, Ethel first, and skidded into some strange powdery white stuff on the ground.

"It's wet," said Elfreda.

"It's cold," I said.

"It's snow!" shouted Ethel.

CHAPTER NINETEEN

The Prison Farm

I looked around and gasped. The wood was transformed. Tree branches, bushes and patches of ground were covered with a magical shiny white. Only a light sprinkling of snowflakes had managed to find its way through the branches of our beech tree, but not far away was a hollow open to the sky. Snow had settled thickly there, glittering in the moonlight, beckoning us to come and play. It was too inviting to resist.

"Come on!" shouted Ethel.

She scooted across and took a flying leap into the middle of it. Me and Elfreda followed, and we all rolled around and kicked snow over each other as if we were small cubs again.

Suddenly I realised we were being watched. Four foxes were standing on the edge of the hollow. Though it was so long since I'd seen them, I knew them straight away – Dad's sister Alison, her husband Rufus and my cousins Roger and Rowena. Alison and Rufus stood and laughed, but the cousins yelled "Wheeeee!" and leapt into the snow-fight.

"Look at you!" said Mum, poking her head out of their earth. "No one's coming inside till you've got cleaned up."

So we shook ourselves, brushed each other down and trooped back into the heat of the living room, where we crowded round the oven and steamed ourselves dry.

Everyone was delighted to see me, and they were even more pleased to hear that I was coming with them.

"Changed your mind, eh? Fancy a nice plump young bird?" asked Uncle Rufus heartily.

"Absolutely not," said Mum firmly, before I had a chance to say anything. "He's just coming as a lookout."

"I thought I might see you lot last night," I said, anxious to change the subject.

"Oh, Mum persuaded us not to go," said Rowena. "I thought it'd be a laugh, but apparently some animals were killed. And not just mice and rabbits, I mean."

"I wish I could have persuaded Ethel," said Mum. "I knew Elfreda was going to warn Edgar. That was different."

"Oh, and what did I do?" objected Ethel. "Only saved him from being squashed to death by a badger, that's all. And what thanks do I get?"

"It's true, Mum," I backed her up. "She saved my life. Didn't you know?"

Mum looked in surprise at Ethel, who sat smirking at everyone.

"Where are Rupert and Rosalind?" asked Elfreda.

"Partying," said Roger, "but me and Ro thought this looked like more fun."

"Right, that's enough small talk," said Rufus. "Let's get a move on, or it'll be light before we get there."

Then I was one of nine shadows sliding between the trees and across the gleaming fields. What with the moon and the dazzling brightness underfoot, we hardly needed our night eyes. My heart leapt at the joy of running in the cold, bracing air. My nostrils tingled with the smells of the night, subtly changed by this new beautiful thing – snow.

The huge barns stood bleakly in a row, and we chose the nearest one. Rufus had already found the best place to dig, and we hollowed out two tunnels under the fence. With no scent of dogs in the air, and no human houses near, we sauntered round the building looking for a weak spot.

Elfreda found one.

"Look, here's some loose boarding," she whispered.

"Your name isn't Sharpeyes for nothing," said Rufus, winking at her.

I started to feel uneasy again. I really shouldn't have anything to do with this, but it was a bit late to back out now.

Dad and Rufus worried at the boards with their teeth until two came away, leaving a hole big enough to squeeze through.

"What an awful smell," said Mum.

"It doesn't smell much like the other farm," said Rufus, "but the chickens'll taste the same."

Dad was the first to wriggle through and one by one the others joined him, with me staying outside to keep watch. I shouldn't feel too bad about that, I told myself. After all, I wouldn't want anything to happen to my family.

The night was still. No living creature seemed to be moving in the black and silver landscape. Only my breath puffed tiny clouds into the air.

After a minute or so I heard a whisper from Dad.

"Edgar! Come here! Whistling worms, son, you'll never believe this!"

I pushed my way in and waited for my eyes to adjust to the

dim light. The first thing to hit me was the stench. It was warm in here – I could hardly breathe. And what were these peculiar blocks of things everywhere? They seemed to be made of webbing, like a spider's web but straight up and down and across. And the webbing was hard – thin strips of that shiny grey stuff that humans used such a lot. Where were the chickens?

Then I blinked…no…my eyes must be playing tricks on me…this couldn't be true…

"They're cages, son," said Dad in my ear. "Little prison cells."

I'd never heard of cages, but I knew what a prison was. It was a hole you had to go in when you'd done something very bad, while the Great Stag thought what to do with you. No one stayed in there for long – just until the Stag decided whether to send you away or get you to do some work to make up for whatever wrong you'd done.

Now I was looking at row upon row of cages piled on top of each other. Stacks and stacks of little prison cells. And in each cage were not one prisoner, nor two, but four or five hens squashed together, with no room to turn round. Had they all done something wrong? And would they ever be allowed out?

The prisoners were nothing like the hens at the other farm, fat and healthy, fluffing up their feathers and strutting round as if the farm belonged to them. These looked sick and listless, as if they'd been shoved in here to die. Sores showed red and angry on the bare patches between their feathers. As for strutting – they had no room even to stretch their wings.

We all walked around, gaping in disbelief.

I felt as if I were in a nightmare. This was worse than death. It was torture. I sat down and gazed at the birds in pity. If only I could do something for them! The chickens peered hopelessly back through the hard grey webbing. Foxes, they seemed to be thinking – so? What could be worse than this?

I could see clearly now, and the more I saw, the less I could believe it. The birds seemed to be standing on the bare criss-crossed strips, with nothing to protect their feet. I crept closer. Just above my eye level was a scraggy hen who looked more dead than alive. There was something wrong with her claw. It was tangled up in the webbing. Tangled up and she couldn't get it free! Now and again it would twitch, but she seemed to have almost given up.

Her cellmate was luckier. Squashed against the first one, she'd somehow found a cushion to rest on. A cushion with straggly feathers and bits of blood on it. My stomach heaved. She was sitting on a dead hen! A corpse cushion!

The air stank of rotting bodies and the droppings of hundreds of chickens. Suddenly I couldn't bear it any longer. I dived for the hole.

"Humans," I heard Mum say in disgust. "Unbelievable!"

Then I heard my Aunt Alison. "There's nothing fit to eat in here. Let's go and leave the poor wretches. We would have given them a quick death, not this."

They all squeezed back through the hole after me, gulping in the cold, fresh air outside.

I loped home with my mind whirling. Somebody should pay for this! The monsters who did this should suffer! If only I could lock them up in cages with no room to move and leave them there! The beauty of the snow only made it worse. Those birds would never see the snow, or the sky or the sun shining.

"The Great Stag ought to know about this," said Rufus grimly, when we reached home.

"What can *he* do about it?" snorted Dad.

I didn't know, but I did know this. *Somebody* would have to do *something*!

CHAPTER TWENTY

Putting Your Back Paw In It

Word about the new chicken farm galloped through the wood. I think the Stag would soon have heard even if Rufus hadn't made a point of telling him. The other Horn Wooders couldn't believe it any more than we could. A few made the journey to see for themselves and told everyone that, yes, it really was true.

I decided to stay two more days with Mum and Dad, until the badgers' meeting with the Lord of the Wood. I kept well away from the Stag, though. I was all too aware that I shouldn't be there, and I didn't fancy being thrown out again.

I spent my last morning sniffing around with Elfreda, still enjoying the sights and smells of my old home. Despite everything that had happened – Cuthbert, and the chicken farm – it was hard not to enjoy being with my family.

Straight after breakfast we headed for a part of the wood where we felt safe from seeing the Stag. The tree boughs hung low here and a deer could easily get his antlers caught in the branches.

"It's a shame the snow didn't last a bit longer," said Elfreda, as we ploughed through mounds of slush. Last year's leaves mixed with melted snow made a messy ground covering.

"Sh!" I whispered. "That's not…is it?"

It was. Picking his way delicately towards us, head down to keep his antlers free, was the last person I wanted to see.

I froze. What was the Stag doing here? Dad said he hardly ever came here. Was it too late to hide? I'd just decided to make a bolt for it when the Stag looked up. Our eyes met. Then he calmly and deliberately went on walking towards us.

"Oh, Edgar!" squeaked Elfreda.

The Stag came to a halt right in front of us. There was a moment's silence. I went hot all over, remembering the things I'd yelled after the battle.

"Good morning, Sharpeyes brother and sister," said the Stag at last.

"Good morning, your grace," we mumbled, and stood as if waiting for our doom. But the Lord of the Wood, it seemed, wanted to talk.

"I have been visiting the Chief of the Badger Clan, who has been unwell. I could enquire what you are doing here…" He paused and put his head on one side.

I opened my mouth. No sound came out, so I shut it again.

"But no matter," continued the Stag. "There is something I want to ask you."

Elfreda and I looked sideways at each other. What on earth could he want?

"Your Uncle Bushytail called to tell me about your hunting expedition. I must say that I was shocked beyond words to hear of the imprisonment of these birds. What I want to know is, was it really as bad as your uncle described? He has been known to – er – exaggerate on occasion."

"Well, he wasn't exaggerating this time – it was terrible," said Elfreda, gathering her courage. "No animal would ever do that to another creature. They looked so ill, and so hopeless."

The Stag shook his head.

"Humans," he said gravely. "I shall never understand them."

I thought once again of the rows of caged chickens, squashed together, sick, with nothing to live for.

"Can't *you* do something about it?" I pleaded.

"I fear not," answered the Stag. "My power does not extend beyond the edge of this wood."

I looked up at him. What did he mean? Then why had he encouraged the Horn Wooders to invade Badgers' Hollow? That was outside his wood. If he hadn't done that, Cuthbert would still be alive! Something boiled up inside me, just as it had after the battle.

"Well, you conveniently forgot that the other night!" I said hotly. "You accuse *me* of going against nature and throw me out of the wood, just because I don't want to kill anyone, but when something like this happens, and humans go against nature in that horrible, horrible way – and no animal'd ever *dream* of doing stuff like that – *then* it seems there's nothing you can do about it."

I stopped, shocked at my own words, and shrank back. What was I doing? The Stag had been trying to be friendly with me, and yet again I'd made a mess of things! And after all, what could a deer do against humans? I hung my head. I could feel Elfreda frozen beside me.

The Stag paused, then without changing either his expression or the tone of his voice, he replied.

"I am sorry to disappoint you, Sharpeyes. I wish that my powers were as great as my responsibilities. Remember me to your esteemed parents. And now I must be gone. I have much to do."

He bowed his head and continued on his way, antlers low and hooves picking their way carefully through the slush.

Astonished, we bowed in turn and stood watching him go. Then Elfreda rounded on me.

"What's the matter with you? Every time you meet him you open your mouth and put your back paw in it! He was actually trying to be friendly. I mean, you're not even supposed to *be* here till the Autumn Offering, and he is the Lord of the Wood, you know."

"I know, I know," I groaned. "There's just something about him that makes me react like that. It was when he said that bit about his power not extending outside this wood, and I thought how he'd encouraged that hunting raid all the way out to Badgers' Hollow, and then Cuthbert got killed."

Elfreda shook her head.

"Hiccupping hedgehogs, Edgar! You like living dangerously, don't you!" she said. "I was amazed he reacted so well. I thought he'd at least say you could never come back again."

"So did I," I agreed. "I must learn to shut up. And we must be careful tonight, when we're eavesdropping."

That evening I said goodbye to my family. With lots of promises to take care of myself and see them soon, I set off with Elfreda for the death-strip tunnel.

I hadn't been invited to this meeting so I planned to hide, listen to the conversation and join up with the badgers afterwards. Elfreda was curious too, and besides, it was a bit of an adventure.

We soon left the trees and started across the fields that led to the death-strip. The moon, although now beginning to wane, was still bright, and shed a white light over everything.

"Does this remind you of something?" I asked as we padded along.

"When you left before, you mean, and we weren't quite sure where you were going, and then we met Aidan? Seems like years ago, doesn't it, not just a few moons."

"I'm glad you're my sister, Elfreda," I said. "You're so…" I searched for the right word, but all I could come up with was, "well, you're always there."

"Thanks a lot," said Elfreda. "Makes me sound really exciting."

We'd set out early, so we reached the tunnel well before the others and searched about for somewhere to hide. We were looking for a bush big enough to crawl under and down-wind of the meeting place, so no one would catch our scent. Once we found one we wriggled around, made ourselves as comfortable as we could, and waited…and waited.

CHAPTER TWENTY-ONE

Eavesdropping

"What's taking them so long?" whispered Elfreda. "This branch is sticking in me."

"I don't know," I whispered back. "I hope we've got the right night. It's not very comfortable here, is it? I wonder……"

"Sh!" hissed Elfreda urgently.

There was a rustle and the sound of twigs and undergrowth being delicately trodden on. Then the Stag and his Lady Hind stepped into view. They were followed by four other deer, two male and two female, all looking warily around. The Lady wore her winter crown of shiny evergreen leaves.

When they were satisfied that they were alone, they came and stood in a semicircle, a little way from the tunnel entrance – and right by our hiding place!

All I could see now was a forest of legs and, between them, the dark mouth of the tunnel. The deer stood quietly, the Stag sometimes murmuring something to his Lady. Up above us, the odd zoom-hound whizzed past, but there were long gaps of almost silence.

My breathing suddenly sounded very loud to me. My back

started to itch, but I daren't move a muscle. I was aware of Elfreda beside me, wide-eyed, her breathing shallow with excitement and sounding even louder than mine.

Had this really been a good idea?

A few unbearable minutes later, a fox's pointed nose appeared at the tunnel entrance. It was Hugo, who had a good look and sniff round before signalling to someone in the tunnel. Mildred and Edith came next, warily sniffing the air like Hugo.

I could make them out quite clearly between the deer's legs. I waited…no Harold.

Edith came up to the Stag and his Lady and bowed gravely. All the deer bowed in return. Then she spoke.

"I received a message that you wished to meet me and my husband. I apologise for his absence, but he's unable to travel. Some of your weasels attacked him the other night, and he's in bed now with a high fever. To tell you the truth, it's touch and go whether he lives or not. I can't stay long – I didn't like leaving him."

The Hind gasped, and a chill shadow fell across my heart. I'd thought Harold would be all right after a good night's sleep.

"I am truly sorry to hear this," replied the Stag. "You will probably not believe how sorry I am. It adds to the burden of guilt which I already carry."

"Well, I'm glad you're sorry, sir," said Edith matter-of-factly, "but that won't make Harold better. Our healer Osbert, my son-in-law, has done all he can for him, and he's also carrying a burden – of grief. Tell him, Hugo."

Hugo stepped forward.

"Osbert's brother, Cuthbert, was killed by two stoats from your wood the other night. Admittedly he had killed their brother, but only when he was defending our friend Edgar Sharpeyes. This stoat went for Edgar's throat, and Cuthbert killed him when he pulled him off. The stoat's two sisters saw that and killed Cuthbert in revenge."

This was worse and worse. The shadow tightened its grip on me, as I struggled to make sense of it all.

I hadn't realised that Cuthbert had died coming to my defence. So it was my fault, in a way. And what had I been doing, enjoying myself with my family when Harold might be dying? Suppose I didn't get back in time to say goodbye to him!

"We think, sir," said Edith, "that you have a lot to answer for, and we'd like to hear what you have to say."

The Stag drew himself up to his full height and waited for a few seconds before replying.

"I called you here," he began, "to apologise for our attack. This is the first winter since the digging of the death-strip tunnel. Many in Horn Wood felt that we should extend our winter hunting grounds. Mistakenly, I agreed that they could.

"It was meant to be a hunting raid, not a battle. Perhaps we should have realised how fiercely you would defend your land, but we did not. Our losses were greater than yours, but we recognise that we brought them on ourselves.

"Will you make a treaty of friendship with us, and let us agree that this will never happen again?"

"Well, it certainly won't happen from our side," said Edith, "but how do we know we can trust you?"

"I have been thinking deeply since the battle," said the Stag. "We have lately received unbelievable news of the cruelty of humans. There is a chicken farm not far from here, I am told, in which the birds are kept squashed together in tiny cages, and never see the sun. That is going against nature to a terrible degree.

"I believed that your ways were wrong, but I see now that, compared to this abomination, you live your lives in harmony with nature, as we do. You simply choose not to kill, except in defence of yourselves and your friends. You do not imprison your fellow creatures.

"As a sign of our good faith, please tell your friend Edgar Sharpeyes that he will be welcome in Horn Wood, and so will anyone who chooses to live as you do. I have to ask you to trust me when I say that we will never attack again."

The three animals from the Hollow put their heads together and didn't take long to decide.

"All right," said Edith. "Let's do it properly, and put our paw and hoof prints somewhere."

Mildred nosed around and found a muddy patch with hardly any grass growing on it. Each animal solemnly left a footprint on it: one badger's paw-mark, two foxes' paw-marks and six hoofprints.

Just as they were turning to leave, the Lady Hind spoke.

"We do hope that your husband recovers. Please tell everyone how truly sorry we are," she said gravely.

Edith nodded curtly and said, "I must be off."

I wanted to leap up and join my friends straight away, but I dared not, while the Stag was still there. The deer spent several minutes talking quietly before they left.

"Well," said Elfreda once they were gone, "you've got no excuse not to visit us now. He's changed, hasn't he, since the Autumn Offering?"

"Yeah," I said, "though he still can't open his mouth without turning it into a speech. But I think he really has learned something. Perhaps that's why he wasn't too angry with me this morning."

I crawled out from under the bush.

"I must go, Elfreda. I'll have to run all the way. I must get back to Harold. See you soon."

One last nuzzle, and I sped off through the tunnel.

As I raced along, the shadow still clutched at my heart. I could just see the other three ahead. Edith was moving quickly for an elderly badger – she must be really anxious to get back to Harold. I didn't want to waste my breath in calling to them, so I concentrated on running.

Why had I stayed so long with my family? Harold had been like a second father to me. I didn't want him to die, and I couldn't bear it if he died without saying goodbye.

And why hadn't I been able to protect Cuthbert? Cuthbert had saved my life – why hadn't I been able to do the same for him? I hadn't even seen him killed. Everything I did seemed to go wrong.

The three animals ahead were taking the easy, but slightly longer route back to the Hollow. It must be because of Edith – Hugo and Mildred would have used the short cut, down a steep wooded hill.

The most important thing was to get back to Harold, so I decided on the short cut. Without slowing my pace, I swerved and started to clamber down the slope, zigzagging between the trees. I had to stop myself falling once or twice, but I got to the bottom in one piece and found myself out of the sparse woodland in an open field.

I was ahead of the other three now and I didn't want to wait for them. Speed was everything! With my mind racing as fast as my legs, I didn't stop to see if the coast was clear. No time for sticking to hedgerows when Harold might be dying.

The night was a blur as I scooted across the middle of the field, my breath rasping in my throat. No time to look for warning signals…

A shot blasted the air.

CHAPTER TWENTY-TWO

Two Meetings

A killing stick! That meant humans! But… I wasn't dead, was I? And *where* was I? I'd been running across the middle of a field and now I was…lying under a hedge?

How had I got there? Had I flown? And what was this thing pinning me down?

Another shot nearly shattered my eardrums, and made every nerve in my body quiver.

"Don't move," whispered a voice in my ear. "Keep absolutely still and you'll be all right."

I managed to turn my head slightly, and found myself held in the gaze of a pair of enormous liquid eyes. The creature had a curious, silvery shimmer about her, but the paw holding me down felt as solid as a rock. I knew her at once, though I'd never seen her before.

It was the Spring Hare.

She lay quite still beside me, her long ears flat down her back. Far bigger than an ordinary hare, she had a long-limbed grace even lying in this awkward position.

My breathing slowed down. My heart gradually stopped

pounding. I just lay there and stared at her, while the panic ebbed out of me. I felt as if I were a small cub again, listening to Mum telling a story. Ethel hadn't believed in the Spring Hare, but I had. Or I'd wanted to believe. If only I could see her, I remembered thinking.

The Hare gazed at me, unblinking, and I felt that she could see right inside me. A deep feeling of calm spread through me.

Then I heard a human voice shouting. Once again I tensed. The voice was harsh, almost like a crow cawing, but I could make out the words.

"Did you get it, Bill?"

"Nah. Must have missed it. Can't see a body, anyway. Ruddy foxes. I'll get it next time!"

The Hare put her paw to her muzzle. "Sh!" she breathed.

The voices faded away until everything was silent and that wonderful deep calm filled me again. I couldn't take my eyes off her.

"I thought you only came in springtime," I whispered.

She relaxed her surprising rock-hard grip and pointed to a tiny white flower, petals closed for the night, just in front of my nose.

"The first snowdrop of spring," she said. "You can sit up now."

"Thank you," I murmured. "Thank you."

Then a thought came to me.

"Can I ask you another favour? I know it's a cheek, when you've just saved my life, but my friend Harold's ill. Can you help him?"

"I am aware of this already," said the Hare. "All creatures must die, you know. Death is a part of life. I have paid him a visit tonight, but do not ask any more. And now, little fighter, *I* have a request."

I sat open-mouthed. What could *she* possibly want of *me*?

"I want you to try being kind to yourself. When you're not blaming the Great Stag for everything, you seem to spend all your time blaming yourself. I want you to remember that sometimes things just happen, and it's not always somebody's fault. Now go. I thought you were in a hurry."

And I found myself running towards the Hollow. I skidded to a halt and turned round to thank her once again. But she was gone.

My paws seemed to have grown wings – I was flying over the ground without any effort at all. It felt like only a few seconds before I was racing into the entrance of Harold and Edith's sett. Then I pulled myself up sharply and crept down the passage to the main bedroom.

The room was lit by the dim glow of a partly covered lantern. Harold lay quite still on the low wooden bed, with two figures beside him. Facing me sat the familiar stocky shape of Osbert, but this side of the bed was the slender back and bushy tail of a stranger – a vixen by her scent.

Osbert stood up in surprise.

"Edgar! I'm so glad you're back. I don't think you know Mildred's sister, Marian. She's been helping out while you've been away."

The visitor turned round, and I looked into the golden eyes of the most beautiful young vixen I had ever seen.

CHAPTER TWENTY-THREE

Fricasseed Field Mice

Harold stirred and mumbled something. Osbert turned back and put his paw to Harold's forehead. Then he nodded.

"Cooler," he whispered.

Harold opened his eyes.

"Where is she?" he asked.

"Who?" asked Osbert.

"The Spring Hare," he murmured. "She gave me such a lovely cool drink."

Osbert smiled.

"Your fever does seem to have left you," he said. "But I think you've been dreaming, old friend. There's been no one here but us."

"Yes, she was here," insisted Harold. "It felt too real to be a dream. And where's Edith?"

I tiptoed over to the bed.

"She's coming," I said. "She wasn't far behind me."

Harold smiled at me peacefully.

"I'll go now," said Marian. "You don't need me any more."

"Oh, don't go," I said, and then felt stupid for saying it.

I was saved by the arrival of a breathless Edith, who took Harold's paw into her own and stroked it. He squeezed hers in response and she plumped herself down on the bed with a huff of relief.

"Well, my dear, what a fright you gave us," she said. "What have you got to say for yourself, eh?"

Once the fever left him and his wound healed, Harold gradually got his strength back. We didn't tell him about Cuthbert until he was well enough to get out of bed. He took it very hard.

At first he hardly spoke about it, but just sat gazing into the fire. Then one day, when me and Edith were keeping him company, he broke his silence.

"It should have been me, not someone so young," he said suddenly. "I'm old and I've had a good life – seen my grandchildren born. He had everything in front of him…and now nothing. It just doesn't make sense."

"I've given up trying to make sense of anything," I told him. "But one thing I do know – you mustn't go feeling guilty about it. That's what the Hare said. Sometimes things just happen, she said, and there's nothing you can do about it and it isn't your fault. There's no way you could have saved Cuthbert, so just be glad you're not both dead."

Edith nodded.

"You're becoming quite a wise young fox," she said.

"Me, wise? You're joking! I've tried to work out what it's all about, but I can't. All you can do is stick to what you think is right, look after your friends and enjoy yourself."

"Sounds quite wise to me," said Harold.

"There are some things, though, that you *ought* to be able

to do something about," I went on. "The trouble is… I just don't know what."

"You mean that chicken farm," said Edith. "That's really bothering you, isn't it?"

"You didn't see it," I said. "However much I try, I can't get across how…how…*see*? I can't even find a word to describe it. Those poor, poor birds." I sighed and shook my head. "I'm going for a walk. Perhaps a bit of fresh air'll clear my head."

"Two heads are better than one," said Edith. "Why don't you call on someone and see if they've got any ideas."

I smiled. "You're so subtle, Edith, I don't think. You know where I'm going, don't you."

Edith smiled back, while Harold looked at us both with a puzzled expression. Climbing the passage to the entrance, I heard him ask, "Where *is* he going?" and Edith chuckle, "Never you mind!"

Once outside, I trotted across the central dell and past the first row of homes on the other side – the ones with entrances facing straight into the dell, like Harold and Edith's sett. My breath formed little clouds in the raw night air and my feet crunched softly on the frosty grass.

I was making for a sett under an elm tree on the outer edge of Badgers' Hollow. It had once belonged to an old badger called Ermintrude, but she'd died peacefully in her sleep just after Hugo came to the Hollow. Her children had moved to Brock Wood, so Hugo moved in. He'd shored up crumbling walls, cleaned out rooms full of dead leaves and goodness knows what else and was busy turning it into an up-to-date foxes' earth.

Mildred was helping him, because this was where they planned to set up home and start a family. And for a while now, the earth had had someone else staying there. She was the reason, as Edith knew, for my visit.

The scent of hot chestnuts wafted up towards me as I trotted down the passageway. I'd already eaten, but they did smell good!

"Hello! Got any left?" I greeted them.

Nobody answered. Hugo and Mildred were sitting bolt upright, glaring at each other from either side of their newly built stone oven.

"What? Oh, hello, Edgar," muttered Hugo. "Yes, help yourself."

Mildred nodded at me and pushed a bowl in my direction. A few blackened chestnuts sat in the bottom.

"Er – well, I won't stay if you're discussing something important," I mumbled, though neither was saying a word to the other.

"Oh, it's nothing important," said Mildred. "Just Hugo getting things totally out of proportion."

"Huh!" barked Hugo. "Oh no, it's not important! It's just the entire reason for the existence of Badgers' Hollow! It's just the only reason I live here and not in the Wood! It's only what we were all fighting for, and what Cuthbert died for!"

Mildred sprang up on to all fours.

"That's not fair!" she yelled. "I fought too, and I still would, to protect everybody! I'd give anything to have been able to save Cuthbert!"

"Calm down, calm down," I said. "I'd better go, but I don't want you at each other's throats. You're two of my very best friends!"

Hugo was on his feet now as well. He and Mildred looked as though they were about to attack each other. I didn't know what to do.

"Erm – where's Marian?" I asked.

"Being a coward and keeping out of the way," said a soft voice behind me.

I melted. Surely everything would be all right now that she'd appeared.

"Let's sit down and explain what it's all about," she went on. "Come on, Edgar. Come and sit by the oven."

Marian went and sat between Hugo and Mildred and beckoned me to follow. I glanced nervously at Mildred and then joined them. Slowly Hugo sat on his haunches and at last Mildred did the same.

"Good," said Marian. "Mildred and I have been home, Edgar, to visit our parents, and while we were there we did what we always do. We ate the sort of food we grew up with – cooked animals."

"Fricasseed field mice," put in Mildred. "Mum cooked it because she knows it's my favourite."

Marian looked at me and waited for my reaction. "Are you shocked?"

I gulped. I was. I could no more sit down to a dish of fricasseed field mice than I could tuck into roast fox. Hugo and Mildred were both staring at me.

"Well, you're surprised, at any rate," said Hugo with some satisfaction. "I can see you are."

"I ate it because I didn't want to put Mum to any extra bother," said Marian, "but I am starting to feel uncomfortable about it, so next time..."

"Well I'm not," Mildred butted in. "When in Brock Wood, do as the Brock Wooders do and when in Badgers' Hollow...but Hugo hadn't realised that's how I feel until I mentioned it tonight. And that's what all the fuss is about."

"But I didn't *say* anything!" objected Hugo.

"You didn't have to!" said Mildred. "Your face was enough!" She turned to me. "Hugo's got this wonderful romantic idea about all animals living in peace and harmony with each other, but nature's not like that. I mean, obviously I wouldn't want to eat someone I knew, like Isabel, but sometimes when I'm scrabbling around for nuts to eat and I see a whole troop of wood mice filing past, I think, well, wouldn't it make life easy if I could pop a few of them in the pot."

"Mildred!" exploded Hugo. "If you feel like that, perhaps you'd better go back to Brock Wood to live!"

"Oh, whistling worms, I wouldn't actually do it! But there are so *many* of them. And it would help the overcrowding problem."

"This is clan-folk we're talking about, not vegetables!" said Hugo. He looked really hurt.

"I know, I know," said Mildred, who was obviously calming down. "And I'd never actually kill anyone – unless I was being attacked, or my friends were. But I just can't promise never to eat an animal that someone else has cooked. They taste so nice!"

Ever since Mildred had mentioned helping with the overcrowding I'd been stifling a giggle. I didn't know why. It didn't seem appropriate at all, but now I couldn't stop myself and a cross between a snort and a guffaw forced itself out of my mouth.

Hugo gaped at me, but Mildred and Marian grinned.

"I'm sorry," I gasped, trying to control myself. "I know this is deadly serious, but you do make it sound funny, Mildred." I cleared my throat. "You're making me think. I can see that it's easy for me because I don't like the taste of animals. Ever since meeting Robbo when we were little, I've had a sort of horror of eating them. And you, Hugo, you've been playing in the Hollow since you were tiny, so you've always had all sorts of animals as friends. But these two haven't, so it's harder for them."

Mildred nodded. "I only came here because of you, Hugo, but I can see that it's a good way to live. I've promised never to kill an animal for food, but don't ask me to go further. This is my home now and I'll stick by the rules and fight to the death to defend everyone, but I'm not going to give up Mum's fricasseed field mice!"

We all looked at Hugo. He shuffled around a bit and gave Mildred a little half-smile. Finally, he said, "It's a deal!"

Mildred laughed. "That's big of you," she said. "Honestly, you were looking at me as if I'd done something really wicked, like those chicken farmers Edgar told us about. Now that *is* evil!"

"Well, that's something we can agree on!" said Hugo.

"It's not farmers, it's just one farmer," said Marian. "Benedict was telling me about him. Apparently he lives near here and our farmers want his land, but he won't let them have it."

"Really?" I said, sitting bolt upright. "That *is* interesting! How does Benedict know?"

"Oh, owls know all sorts of things," said Hugo. Then he opened his eyes very wide and put his head on one side, like an owl.

"Owls know a thing or twooo," he hooted, "but we keep our counsel, we dooo, we dooo."

We all shrieked with laughter, it was so like the Hootingly-ffeatherclaw cousins. Hugo stood on his hind legs and bowed.

"For my next impression..." he said.

"Robbo, Robbo!" shouted Mildred. "Do Robbo!"

Hugo sat up and held his front paws close to his chest. Then he twitched his nose and tried to stick his front teeth out.

Marian was in tears, she was laughing so much, and me and Mildred were rolling round on the floor.

"It jest ain't fair," trilled Hugo in as high a voice as he could manage. "It shoulda been me seein' the Spring Hare." Twitch, twitch. "Hares an' rabbits is like family." Another twitch. "It shoulda been me, not a fox and a badger – mos' def!"

"Oh, don't," gasped Mildred. "I can't bear it!"

I was laughing as much as the others, but all the while my mind was racing. So the prison farmer lived nearby, did he, and he didn't want anyone else to have his land?

And that was when I started to have the beginnings of a plan.

CHAPTER TWENTY-FOUR

Peace with the Enemy?

At first my idea seemed so ridiculous that I didn't mention it to anyone. How could animals manage to do such a thing?

But when I finally plucked up courage to tell Marian she said, with shining eyes, "Oh, Edgar, you're brilliant!"

This made me feel, firstly that anything was worth it to have her looking at me like that, and secondly that it just had to work or I'd be letting her down.

The next person to be consulted was Edith.

"Erm – Marian and I have been thinking about that chicken farmer."

When I'd finished explaining, Edith nodded. "See, I told you two heads were better than one," she twinkled. "I think we need another moot. It'll do Harold good to have something to think about."

So exactly one full moon after the last moot, the Badgers' Hollow dell was once again filled with animals eager to know what it was all about. Edgar and Marian sat at the front this time, with Harold, Edith, Hugo and Mildred. It was a lively meeting, too. Everyone seemed to have an idea of what they'd like to do to the chicken farmer.

"Make a tiny cage and stick him in it!" shouted Henrietta Whitescut, hopping enthusiastically around the dell.

"And how are you going to do that?" asked her grandfather, Henry.

"Yes, practical suggestions only, please," said Harold.

"I could sit on his face and squash him to death," growled Algie, who was the biggest badger I'd ever seen. "Is that practical enough for you?"

A number of animals cheered, but Edith shushed them.

"Even if you could, Algie, we don't want blood on our hands."

"That's right," agreed Harold. "We don't want to sink to his level. Edgar's plan is manageable – I think – but not easy. We're going to need a lot of animals. What we really want to know is, how many of you would be willing to help?"

Every single mouse, rabbit, vole, hedgehog, squirrel, mole and badger sent up a resounding shout of, "I will!"

I felt tears come to my eyes, but not tears of sadness this time. These kind and courageous animals, my friends, all cared this much about some chickens they'd never seen. I turned to Marian. She had that shining-eyed look again. It had got to work!

Several animals were calling out, "When do we get started?"

"Well, not straight away, unfortunately," I said. "There's a problem I've only just thought of. You see, the farmer's house is this side of the death-strip – nice and easy for us. But the chicken farm is on the other side. Now, we could get there using the tunnel, which was my original idea, but we'd be stretching ourselves a bit thin."

Harold and Edith glanced at each other and nodded.

"I can guess what you're thinking," said Harold, "and I say, go for it!"

The audience looked puzzled. Obviously, most of them *couldn't* guess what I was thinking.

Edith gazed round at them all, stamped her forepaw on the ground and said, "The Horn Wooders!"

There was a gasp, then everyone started talking at once.

"What? That scurvy crew?"

"The mob that attacked us?"

"Never! We don't need them!"

"What about the Brock Wooders?" piped up Isabel. "They're our friends."

"Wrong side of the death-strip," said Robbo.

"Doesn't matter," declared Isabel. "If a whole load of animals can come this way from Horn Wood, then a whole load of animals can travel the other way, from Brock Wood."

There was a general murmur of agreement. I'd been feeling more and more uncomfortable as I listened to them all. There was so much I wanted to say, but could I find the right words?

Harold and Edith were talking in low voices.

Then Harold boomed out, "Hush, everyone, please!"

Everyone hushed except some rabbits at the back, who carried on with their lively discussion.

Robbo sat up on his hind legs and glared at them indignantly. This had no effect except to make me and Marian giggle: he looked so like Hugo's impression of him.

Finally he took a deep breath and bawled, "Shut up, you lot!"

They shut up.

"Thank you, Robbo. Thank you, everyone," said Harold mildly.

"Now, before you start calling animals a 'scurvy crew', I think you ought to remember that Edgar comes from Horn Wood and that his family still lives there."

"Yes, but his family didn't join in the attack," squeaked a wood mouse. "I happen to know that his sisters only came to stop him being hurt."

She sat down hurriedly, looking at the same time proud of being in the know and amazed at her own daring in speaking at a moot.

"We've got nothing against Edgar's family," said a hedgehog. "It's the rest of 'em we don't like."

"Hear, hear!" called a lot of voices.

"Let's get this straight," said Edith. "You're saying that every single animal that lives in Horn Wood, apart from the Sharpeyes family, is unworthy of helping us in our plan?"

Cries of, "Yeah! That's right!" and murmurs of, "More or less."

"And what about all the many, many animals from Horn Wood who *didn't* attack us that night?" said Harold. "And the ones who came along unthinkingly for the fun, and regretted it once they got here?"

For the first time, Marian spoke. "Are they all going to be our enemies forever, or are we going to give them a second chance?"

"Well, what about the Great Stag?" said a young rabbit. "As far as I can make out, it was his fault in the first place."

"Ah," said Harold gravely. "Now we come to it. The Great Stag." He paused and looked around at everyone. "It would, of course, be impossible to involve the Horn Wooders without asking the Great Stag. I wasn't well enough to meet with him after the battle, but my good wife did, and Hugo and Mildred. I believe there were also one or two *unofficial* presences at that meeting." He glanced at me with a glimmer of a smile in his eyes. "Hugo, perhaps you'd like to fill everyone in."

Hugo stood up. "Well, the Stag's sorry, I can tell you that.

There've been loads of rumours going round and it's true, he's sorry. Apparently, he thought the tunnel being dug meant they could all just extend their hunting grounds."

"I still find that amazing," said Mildred. "It goes against all the ancient territorial laws. I thought he was so keen on tradition."

"But there are," said Hugo, "such a *lot* of small animals here, as we said at the last moot. I think he felt that living like this put us outside the ancient laws."

I stood up. "I know Hugo's right. And he's a bit blinkered, the Stag. It just didn't occur to him that we'd fight to protect them. He's not used to animals behaving like that. He was shocked there was a battle. I think he assumed we'd just sit back and let everyone be slaughtered."

There was a lot of murmuring at this and then Henrietta Whitescut stood up and coughed. "A lot of us young ones don't know what it's like livin' anywhere else. I'd like to say this has made me feel very grateful to be livin' in Badgers' Hollow among such a kind and brave lot of animals."

She sat down to great cheers and it was some time before Hugo could begin again.

"Now, listen," he said. "There was something else that's made the Stag think again. It's the very thing that we've met here to discuss. When he heard about this chicken farm he was horrified. He said it made us lot look really reasonable, or words to that effect."

I felt I had something important to say. I came from Horn Wood, I'd seen the chicken farm, I'd heard what the Great Stag had said, I'd thought of a plan and now it was up to me to start putting it into action. But I felt nervous.

"Friends," I said, rising to my feet.

Everyone looked at me. I suddenly found that my throat needed a great deal of clearing.

"Er, with your permission, I'd like to go and talk to the Great Stag."

No one said a word.

"Look, he wants to make peace with us. He's not a bad animal and he'd love to help put an end to this evil farm. It has to be me, I think, not Harold or Edith. I've been pretty rude to him more than once, and he still said it would be okay for me to go back and live there. Not that I want to live anywhere but here. Anyway – what do you think?"

The discussion went on for several minutes. Clearly there were a lot of strong feelings. I said nothing more to anyone, but just sat wondering whether I had the nerve to face the Stag again. Then I became aware that a badger was standing at the edge of the crowd, also saying nothing, waiting for quiet. Gradually everyone else realised he was waiting and realised, moreover, who he was. A hush fell.

"I'm sorry for your chickens, Edgar," said Osbert. "I would have helped. But I'm afraid I'm not yet ready to forgive. If you're going to involve the Great Stag you'll have to do it without me. This is just the sort of adventure that Cuthbert would have thrown himself into, but you'll have to do it without *him*, as well. Good luck, everyone, and goodnight." He turned and waddled off to his sett.

I felt as if someone had thrown a pumpkin of cold water over me.

CHAPTER TWENTY-FIVE

Spies

All eyes followed Osbert, and even when he'd vanished into his sett no one said anything. I was profoundly grateful when Harold cleared his throat. Somebody ought to say something, decide something, but I seemed to have lost all power of thought, let alone speech.

"It is very understandable that Osbert should feel like that," said Harold. "Very understandable." He paused for so long that I thought that was all he was going to say. "But the rest of us have a decision to make." Another long pause. "Edgar, are you still willing to approach the Great Stag?"

I nodded. "If you think it's a good idea."

"We must put it to the vote, then," said Harold. "Remembering the suffering of these hens that Edgar has told us about, but bearing in mind what the Horn Wooders did to us, are you willing to involve them in our plan? If you are, raise a paw now."

I stopped breathing as a few paws were raised, then a few more, then a lot more, until finally nearly every animal seemed to have a paw in the air. My breath came out with a whoosh as

I suddenly wondered whether I should raise my own paw. It seemed silly – everyone knew where I stood – but I raised it anyway.

"I've given up counting," said Edith. "Just raise your paw if you're against, now."

About ten animals stuck their paws in the air.

All the moles were at the front, probably because they couldn't see very well, I thought.

One of them suddenly stood up and said, "Several of us moles didn't put our paws up either time, 'cos we can't make up our minds."

"All right, Magnus," said Edith. "All those who don't know or don't mind either way, stick up your paw now."

There were about twenty don't knows.

"Motion carried," called Harold. "And unless there are any violent objections, I'm going to bed."

"Who's going to tell Osbert?" whispered Mildred.

As if in answer to her question, Emma came up to the group at the front.

"Don't worry about Osbert," she said. "He hasn't come to terms with losing Cuthbert. I'll look after him. Once the pain is a little less raw, I know he'll agree with what you're doing."

"Yes, you look after him, dear," said Edith. "He's a good badger, a really kind animal. I'm sure he'll come round to our way of thinking."

It was a few days later that I found myself in a clearing in Horn Wood, waiting for an audience with the Stag. I was nervous, of course I was nervous, and determined not to lose my temper or say anything rude. I'd put it off for as long as I could. First I said that we should work out the plan in more detail. When that was done I paid a visit to my family. But now I couldn't think of any more excuses.

I'd been asked to wait here by a young stag, who'd gone to fetch his lord. I looked around and shivered. Not the weather to be standing still in the open. Most of the trees were still bare, but a single tall holly bush brightened the clearing with its berries, little blots of crimson against the dark green leaves. They cheered me up a bit. To give myself something to do, I started to count them.

By the time the young deer returned with another attendant and the Great Stag himself, I'd counted the berries several times, getting a different number on each occasion.

As the Stag approached, I bowed low. I didn't look up until I heard my name spoken.

"Sharpeyes, I hear you wish to speak with me."

"Well, yes…your grace…erm…first of all I want to apologise… I've been a bit rude to you in the past and I hope you'll forgive that and not hold it against me… I mean, I hope you won't say no to my suggestion just because it's me saying it."

I stopped. This was coming out all wrong.

"Look at me, Sharpeyes," said the Stag.

I looked. Was that a gleam of amusement in the Stag's eyes?

"In the past," said the Stag, "neither of us has been completely fair to the other. I suggest we let bygones be bygones and that you tell me why you have come to see me."

"Well," I said again, and realised that my breath had been coming very fast and that now it was slowing down to normal. "Well, you know that chicken farm…" and I explained my plan to the Stag.

As we talked we walked slowly round the clearing. The two deer attendants stood quite still at the edge and watched us.

The Stag nodded his head as he listened and asked all kinds of questions.

"And are all the animals of Badgers' Hollow in agreement with this? I know they have some strange system of asking everyone's opinion."

"They all want to help the chickens," I said. I paused, then truthfulness forced me to add, "And most of them think it's a good idea for you lot to help. But not everybody. That badger who got killed – my friend Cuthbert – well, his brother doesn't like the idea of involving the Horn Wooders. And there's a few others, too. But most people are fine about it."

The Stag nodded. "Understandable," he murmured. "But one thing I cannot understand. How is it that animals have come to know the mind and the intentions of humans? This is very strange to me."

"Spies," I said.

"Spies?" said the Stag, and stopped in his tracks. "Explain, please."

"It's birds, mainly," I said. "I used to think it was just owls who knew so much, sort of by magic. But all these birds are great gossips. The house martins who live in our farmers' house..."

"*Our* farmers?" queried the Stag.

"We call them that because we use their farm so much, for milk and vegetables and stuff, and they don't seem to be too bad – for humans. At least, the animals who live on their farm seem to have quite a nice life."

"Our farmers," murmured the Stag again, and shook his head. "Stranger and stranger."

"Anyway," I carried on, "these house martins listen in to all sorts of conversations, and then they swap stories with their relatives who live under the chicken farmer's roof. And *everything* gets back to Aidan and Benedict. *And* as well as that, some of our wood mice have been chatting to the house mice in our farmers' house, so they can confirm that side of the story."

"Amazing," said the Stag. "Truly amazing." And he started once more to walk slowly around the clearing.

"One of the most important things the chicken farmer said," I went on, anxious to use every argument I could to persuade him, "was that it wasn't as if his farm was a tumble-down shack. He said it was an up-to-date, state-of-the-art factory farm, and he might let our farmers have it if they offered him more…money?… Whatever that is. But I don't think our farmers have got more money. But if the farm *was* a tumble-down shack, then perhaps he'd let them have it, we thought. And we thought, if his *house* was a tumble-down shack as well, perhaps he'd just go right away."

The Stag said nothing, but carried on at a stately pace around the clearing. I walked with him. I didn't dare ask for a decision in case I got the wrong answer. Finally, when I'd almost given up and started to think about other things like what Mum would be cooking for supper, the Stag stopped walking and looked at me.

"It is a very risky undertaking," he said gravely. "Animals may lose their lives. But more than that, I am not at all sure that your plan will succeed."

My heart sank. We'd have to do it without the Horn Wooders.

"However," said the Stag, "considering the terrible nature of the birds' imprisonment, it may be worth the risk."

I gasped. "Then you'll help us?" I whispered.

"We will help you," agreed the Stag.

CHAPTER TWENTY-SIX

Squiggles

Work started straight away, but it was many days and nights before we were ready for the final push. Days and nights of back-breaking work, worry, exhaustion – and a lot of fun.

At first I tried to be in two places at once, trekking back and forth between the Badgers' Hollow workings and the Horn Wood project. Getting rid of the farmer, satisfying though it would be, felt like a bit of a sideshow. The really important stuff – rescuing the chickens – seemed to be happening on the other side of the death-strip.

"You've got to stop this, Edgar," said Marian. "You'll drop dead from exhaustion. Choose! Are you working with us or them?"

"Yeah, sounds like Elfreda's doing a brilliant job," said Hugo. "Leave it to her."

Elfreda *was* doing a brilliant job. She'd risen to the challenge and shown all sorts of talents: organisation, tact, courage, and the ability to get very different sorts of animals to work together.

"I know what you're thinking," Marian went on. "*You* think the chicken farm's more important than what *we're* doing."

I smiled at her. "You're a mind-reader," I said.

"Look at it this way," put in Mildred. "If we destroy the chicken farm but leave that evil person's house alone, he'll probably go and build another farm just as horrible as the last one. We've got to give him a really nasty shock. Make him want to go away and never see another chicken farm in his life."

"So what we're doing," said Hugo, "is just as important as the Horn Wooders' job."

I felt a weight lift off me. I *had* been trying to do too much. Suddenly I knew where I should be. Badgers' Hollow was my home now, and these animals were my dearest friends.

"Okay, okay," I laughed. "You all win. Elfreda can run things over there."

When the work was very nearly finished, a group of us were sitting recovering in Edith's kitchen. She'd heated some blackberry juice and was ladling it into little bowls and mugs. Harold was dozing in the warm glow from the oven.

"We ought to call this something," I said.

"What?" yawned Hugo. "Smells like blackberry juice to me."

"No, this plan! This thing that we're doing."

"How about...getting rid of the rotten, stinky, evil chicken farmer," suggested Mildred.

"Ain't exactly snappy," said Robbo. "Oughtta be *Operation* somethin'."

"Operation *Something*?" snorted Mildred. "That's a stupid title!"

"Duh!" said Robbo. "Not 'Somethin''! I jest couldn't think o' the second word. Gimme time."

"Digging ought to be in the title," suggested Isabel, blowing on her forepaws. "My poor paws! Thank the Hare the weather's turned. Imagine if we'd had to dig through frozen ground!"

"Don't forget the nibblers and gnawers if you're giving it a name," said Edith, "or you'll hurt their feelings."

"Operation Diggin' and Gnawin'," said Robbo. "Nah."

"Benedict suggested we should call the final day 'Demolition Day'," put in Marian.

"Trust an owl to come up with some long word," said Mildred.

"D-Day for short," Marian went on.

"What's D?" I asked.

"Benedict said it's the first bit of 'demolition', when you write it down."

"Excuse my ignorance," said Hugo, "but what does 'demolition' mean, and what does 'write it down' mean?"

"Demolition is knockin' somethin' down," said Robbo importantly. "And…er…'write it down' is…er…"

"You know, it's those squiggles humans put on everything," explained Marian.

I looked at her in admiration. She'd always enjoyed talking to the owls and learning what she could from them.

"I knew that," said Robbo. "About the squiggles."

"Okay, if you're so clever," said Isabel, "why do they do that? Cover things with squiggles?"

"Well, it's…um…to do with…yo, Edith, let me help you."

Robbo leapt up and cupped a bowl of steaming blackberry juice in his paws, then carefully handed it to Marian. Isabel sniffed loudly.

"Thank you, Robbo," said Marian. "I think… I'm not sure, but I think it must be in case they forget the names of things. They write on them to help themselves remember."

There was a general head-shaking, as often happened

when humans were discussed.

"Poor humans," said Edith, "having such bad memories."

A few nights later, I was waiting with a party of diggers in the shadows outside the gate of the chicken farmer's house. Algie was there – they were going to need brute strength tonight – a few more young badgers, a number of rabbits and some moles, mice and voles.

I knew that Isabel and her rabbit friends were quietly at work in the field round the back and Hugo, Mildred, Marian and Robbo were directing four digger parties underground, directly beneath where the farmer lived.

This place had become familiar, but I still shivered whenever I came. The house was squat and ugly, all sharp angles and corners. A sense of menace seemed to hang around everything, even the gateposts. It's just my imagination, I thought. It's only a human house. But still I shivered.

It was a windy night, with dark clouds scudding in front of the half-moon. Good – that would hide any accidental noises. Everyone's senses were as alert as an animal's senses can be, for the chicken farmer was inside.

He was alone. Lights were on at the bottom of the house, but something was pulled across the windows so we couldn't see in. Sometimes he had a female with him, but not tonight. She fascinated me, this female. She was so different from the farmer. Even their back paws were different. His were flat and he could walk on them quite quickly, but hers had vicious-looking spikes at the back, some sort of claw which she had to balance on. They slowed her down, but they must be formidable weapons. Then the fur on her head was long and pale and shiny, while his was short and brown. They were far more different from each other than any dog-fox and vixen.

But the strangest thing was that there was another quite different female who came sometimes in the daytime. I'd caught glimpses of her through the kitchen door, down on all fours like a normal animal, scrubbing the floor. She was old and plump and often made a strange warbling noise, and she didn't have spikes on her back paws. Perhaps she was a different breed of human, just as there seemed to be different breeds of dogs. I liked her. She seemed harmless and she had a homely scent, while the other female's scent was so sickly and overpowering, you could smell it a mile off.

One thing I was very glad about was that there were no cubs, or whatever humans called their young. I would have felt just a little bit mean if there'd been cubs involved.

Now, where was that owl?

Two great wings swooped down and a pair of feathery claws gripped the branch above me.

"Mr P Stoooonehart," hooted Benedict softly. "And a very apt name tooooo."

"How do you know his name?" I said, astonished.

"Shhh!" warned Benedict. "That's what the gate says, don't you knoooow."

I stood quite still and listened hard.

"The gate isn't saying anything," I whispered at last.

"You can see, can't yoooo? The words on the gate, too troooo, too troooo!"

Then I really noticed for the first time what I must have seen many times before. On the gate was a piece of that human, shiny, hard stuff, and cut into it were...squiggles.

The squiggles must have told Benedict the farmer's name!

But why put your own name outside your house? Was his memory really so bad that he might forget it? Or forget, perhaps, that he lived there? And how did Benedict know what the squiggles said?

I looked up at the owl, sitting on his branch gazing about with those enormous round eyes. Who could understand owls, or humans? They lived in different worlds from me and my animal friends. The worlds overlapped, but there must be vast areas of unknown territory. Still, Benedict was a friend, however different.

And suddenly I looked at the squiggles with fresh eyes and knew why the farmer had put them there. Not to remind himself of his own name, but to tell other humans, strangers, that that was the name of the human who lived in this house!

I felt that I'd been down a hole – a nice, comfortable, familiar hole – stuck my head out of the entrance and there was a whole new world waiting to be explored. What an achievement, to work that out all by myself! I'd have to tell Marian as soon as this was over.

I laughed softly to myself. With a bit of luck Mr P Stonehart would soon have to find somewhere else to stick his squiggles.

Suddenly a ripple of excitement flowed through us all. The lights in the house had gone out. Then another light came on higher up. I forgot about squiggles. This second light was usually on for only a short while.

We were all tense, expectant. Sure enough, the house was soon plunged into darkness.

"Hoooo, hoooo," laughed Benedict. "It is, as they say, all systems goooo!"

CHAPTER TWENTY-SEVEN

The Final Push

Benedict's wings flapped a few times as he took to the air, but he wasn't going far. Only to the beech tree in the farmer's garden, from where he'd have a good view of the whole area.

I stood on my hind legs, reached in with my forepaw and unlatched the gate. We were through, but we'd have to be very, very quiet. I fastened the gate back with a boulder and called softly to Algie.

"Ready!" growled Algie and started heaving. He was wearing a harness of plaited ivy and pulling a fallen tree-trunk, which had been dragged all the way from Brock Wood. It wasn't long, but it was really thick. Three young badgers were pushing from behind.

Algie pulled and panted and the others pushed and panted until they'd dragged the trunk up to the front door. Then two wood mice scampered up and bit through the ivy.

"Glad to be free of that," muttered Algie, shaking off the harness.

The next job was to try and wedge the trunk sideways into the porch so that it would block the front door. We'd been careful about the size, but…it was too big.

"Mice and voles!" I whispered urgently, and soon the trunk was swarming with tiny creatures gnawing at the sharp edges that wouldn't quite fit in. I was hopping about with anxiety.

"Don't squash them!" I kept whispering to the badgers, as they slowly pushed the log into place. But the mice and voles were quick. They seemed to know exactly which bits of old wood to work on and always scrambled out of the way before the log was jammed more tightly into the porch.

"There," puffed Algie at last. "I don't think you'll get a tighter fit than that."

"Brilliant!" I said. "Rabbits and moles, do your stuff!"

CRASH!!!

Everyone froze. You could have heard a mouse twitch its tail as we waited, terrified, for a light to flick on, a killing stick to shoot its deadly thunder at someone.

Nothing happened. Praise the Hare, the farmer must be a heavy sleeper. Finally, I allowed my head to move enough to see the cause of the noise.

Two young rabbits were crouching, shaking with fear, by a broken plant pot. I waited a little while longer, then crept over to them.

"It's okay," I whispered. "You can take your paws away from your eyes. How did it happen?"

"We were having a competition," one of them whispered back, "to see who could kick up the biggest pile of earth. I think we got a bit carried away."

"I think you did," I said. "You've frightened everyone to death. I know this is all exciting, but *please* try to be sensible. Our lives depend on it."

The two young rabbits nodded, looking very sorry. I glanced around at the others, still unmoving.

"As I was saying," I whispered, "rabbits and moles, do your stuff. But do it quietly!"

All the while the log was being fitted, the rabbits and moles had been digging a trench in the garden round the front door. They'd kicked the earth on to the house side of the trench, ready for the next stage. That was when the accident had happened.

Now the rabbits started to kick the earth again, on to the log. Their powerful back paws shifted mounds of soil in no time. Then they clambered up and tipped half-pumpkin buckets of earth on to the very top. Finally, they patted it down as hard as they could.

When the chicken farmer opened his door, he'd be able to see over the top, but it would take him ages to push his way out. What we hoped was that he wouldn't bother, but would go straight to the back door.

"It's a good job the ground's not frosty," said a cheerful young rabbit who I recognised as Henrietta, "or I'm not sure we'd have done it."

"I was just thinking," said Algie, "it's a shame we didn't have this much time at the death-strip tunnel. If we'd done this good a job we'd have been able to stop the Horn Wooders coming through."

And Cuthbert needn't have died, I thought, but I didn't say so. You could go mad thinking, *what if, what if*, all the time.

"Well, I must leave you good animals and see how the tunnels are getting on," was what I said instead. "You know your next job, don't you? Remember – make it as difficult as you can for him to come round to the front of the house. We must get him to go out of that back gate. And *be quiet*!"

The farmer's front and back gardens were separated by a wall with a single gate in it. The badgers had got their breath back and were starting to block the gateway. It opened towards the front garden, so they were piling earth and stones up against it on that side.

And what were the rabbits and moles doing now? I grinned as I watched them destroy the garden. They didn't uproot any plants, but the lawn would be a mess of holes and earth by the time they'd finished.

We wanted the farmer to pull back his curtains and rush out of the house. He'd try the front door, find he couldn't get through, go out of the back door and round to his side gate, find he couldn't get through, go to his back garden gate...and there, oh there! What a lovely surprise Isabel would have waiting for him!

I couldn't help laughing as I turned and made for the front gate. When I reached it, I was startled to hear my name called softly.

CHAPTER TWENTY-EIGHT

You Can't Beat a Mole

"Edgar! Halloooo, halloooo!"

Benedict was back on his branch by the gate.

"A prooogress report, from Isabel for yoooo. The cows are doooing very well, they've promised not to moooo. The pit is dug and filling up with lovely brown cow poooo. I'm off, back to that beech tree now, so tooodle-oooo."

I watched the owl glide over to the tree. There he perched, turning his head slowly from side to side, his big yellow eyes surveying both the back and front of the farmer's house.

As I loped along my mind flitted between each group in turn. In some ways Isabel's role was the hardest. All the Badgers' Hollow animals knew they could rely on each other whatever happened. But involving farm animals – that was much trickier. I could never have persuaded the cows to wander across two fields and leave their cowpats in a pit outside the farmer's back gate. But Isabel had a way with these gigantic creatures. They never minded her milking them, and once it was all explained to them the cows felt sorry for the imprisoned chickens. They mooed that they were only too glad to help.

This part of the plan had been Isabel's idea. It had started when she'd remarked how strange it was that the farmer's back gate led directly on to a field, only two fields away from "our" farm. Then the current mild weather had set in and our farmers had let the cows out of the barn to graze until the next cold snap. That's when inspiration had struck her. And according to Benedict, it was all going to plan.

But again and again, as I ran, I thought of the chicken farm. Elfreda's last report, via Aidan, was that everything was going well. If we could only save some of the birds, it would all have been worth it.

My spirits were high as I reached Hugo's tunnel.

"Password," said a rabbit at the entrance.

"Don't be cheeky," I said. "You know who I am."

"I'm only obeying orders," said the rabbit.

"Oh, all right then. Just in case I'm a weasel heavily disguised as Edgar Sharpeyes, the password is D-Day."

"Pass, friend," said the rabbit, and I started down the long, long tunnel.

In the dark I could hear noises, of digging, talking and laughing. It was a relief to be underground, where you didn't have to be quiet. Suddenly the narrow tunnel opened on to a much wider one, almost a room. It went in both directions for a long way. The ceiling was so low that I could just about stand on all fours. Hugo, a few rabbits, mice and voles and a larger number of moles were there, but all this I knew by using my senses of smell and hearing, because I could hardly see a thing.

"Hello, cousin!" said Hugo cheerfully. As he turned to face me his eyes glowed in the almost pitch black. "Just in time for the breakthrough," he went on. "We're nearly through to Mildred's side."

"I thought you'd have had one candle," I said. "I can barely see you, even with my night eyes."

"We did when it was mainly rabbits doing the digging, but the moles are the stars of this bit and they much prefer the dark."

"Hello!" came Mildred's voice suddenly. "I can hear you!"

"Mil!" said Hugo excitedly. He crouched down to the little hole her voice was coming from. "Be careful."

"I'm all right," she laughed. "This is good, isn't it? Listen! We've just got through to Marian's side, but she hasn't quite reached Robbo's yet."

Hugo and Mildred both scrabbled around making the hole bigger, until she could poke her face through. Not that I could exactly see her face. Just two eyes glimmering eerily in the dark.

"Hey, y'all!" called a familiar voice from the other end of the tunnel.

"Robbo!" we shouted.

I ran to help him make his hole bigger, but I'd barely started digging when Robbo managed to squeeze his whole body through.

"We've just reached Marian," said Robbo. "Pretty good job, ain't it?"

I was elated. My plan, which had seemed so complicated and dangerous, was working! One continuous long tunnel now ran beneath all four sides of the farmer's house.

"It's all going well up on top," I told them. "You should see the mess the garden's in! He's going to get the shock of his life when he looks out of his window in the morning."

"Which isn't that far away," said Hugo. "We'd better get a move on. How's it going, Magnus?"

The mole next to us stopped digging.

"Not bad, not bad," he said, and I recognised his scent and voice from the moot.

"Aren't you the mole who didn't know which way to vote?" I asked in my friendliest voice. I didn't want to sound rude.

"That's right," said Magnus. "Us moles like to take our time makin' up our minds. But the more we all thought about it, the more we reckoned it was a good idea. And, meanin' no disrespect, we reckoned you needed us. I mean, there's diggin' and diggin'. I'm not saying you big fellers can't shift a load of earth. But when it comes to the subtle stuff, in tight spaces – well, you can't beat a mole."

"Very true," said Hugo, nodding.

"Oh, absolutely," I agreed.

"So, in answer to your question, Hugo, we're nearly there. In fact, it'll soon be time for all non-moles to skedaddle out of here."

"Already?" I asked.

"You don't want the whole lot collapsin' on top of you now, do you?" said Magnus, as if he were talking to a slightly dim young mole pup. "We don't know how long these walls are gonna stand when they're restin' on just a few columns of earth. It might be a long time or it might be no time at all. Now a mole can dig his way out of almost anythin', but I wouldn't like to say the same for these here rabbits. Or, meanin' no disrespect, your good selves. Come an' have a feel."

I ran my paw over the wall where the moles were working, and felt the difference between the top half and the bottom. The top part felt like roughly baked clay – the foundations of the house, which had been resting securely on the earth beneath.

No longer.

The moles had dug miniature tunnels underneath and removed the supporting earth from both sides. Now the foundations were resting on a few pillars of earth, which were being whittled away to the width of a stick by busy mole paws.

The baked clay wall stopped abruptly at each end of the tunnel and turned a sharp corner.

"I think Magnus is right," said Hugo.

"Course I'm right," muttered Magnus, carrying on with his digging.

"We ought to get these rabbits out of here," Hugo continued. Then, "Mil!" he called urgently through the hole. "Magnus reckons it's getting unsafe. Don't take any chances."

"Yeah, I'm getting the same message from our moles, and so is Marian," said Mildred.

"Thank you, Magnus, and all you wonderful moles," I said from my heart. "Are you sure you'll be safe?"

"Don't you worry 'bout us. We'll hide up somewhere underground. That's where we like best, anyway. You'll see us back in the Hollow in a few weeks, maybe. Now skedaddle off out of it!"

Robbo squeezed back through to his side to have a final check.

"See y'all up top," he said.

"We'll meet up at the entrance by the back of the house," I called to his disappearing white tail.

Then I waved the rest of Hugo's workers up the tunnel and crept up after the last one. Hugo stopped to whisper one last message to Mildred, told the moles to take care, and followed on.

When I poked my nose out of the tunnel the sky was just starting to lighten. I blinked, although the sun was not yet up. It seemed like a bright summer day compared with down below. The wind had dropped while I'd been underground and the morning was still.

The rabbits were sitting in a group rubbing their eyes and

blinking, while the mice and voles were busy cleaning their whiskers.

"Go home, you lot, and stay there," I told them. "Thank you very much for all your hard work, but you must remember to lie low until you hear word that it's safe to move."

They all hopped and scuttled off together, chatting and laughing.

"We should do the same," said Hugo, clambering out of the hole, "but first I'm going to find Mildred."

I opened my mouth to reply but I was stopped by a deafening bellow. It came from the direction of the farmer's house.

CHAPTER TWENTY-NINE

D-Day

Hugo and I grinned at each other. This was too good to miss. Without a word we turned and ran, and found Mildred and Marian already waiting.

This particular tunnel entrance was about half a field away from the farmer's back gate. Robbo, Isabel and a number of other rabbits were there too, all crouched very low in the grass and watching the gate intently.

It was hard to keep as still and quiet as we should when we were all filled with such excited anticipation. I lay in the long grass next to Marian and we both giggled.

"I think we covered it up pretty convincingly," whispered Isabel. "I mean, if you look carefully you'll see it's not quite the same as the grass in the rest of the field, but he's not going to be looking that carefully, I hope."

"Ain't got too hard, has it?" asked Robbo.

"No, I just checked," said Isabel. "The top's crusted over, but there's lots of goo underneath."

There'd been a few bellows from different directions. Now the roaring was coming from the garden. Suddenly we all tensed.

The farmer was by the back gate!

He'd opened it!

We waited. He had something in his forepaw and was holding it up to his ear. Now he'd started talking in a loud, angry voice. I thought I'd never noticed before that the farmer's face was bright red. Perhaps I'd only seen him at night.

"Is there somebody with him?" said Hugo.

"No, I'm sure there's not," said Isabel. "The house has been so closely watched. No one could have got in or out without being seen."

"Well, who's he talking to then?" said Mildred.

"Sh!" I hushed. "See if we can hear what he's saying!"

The farmer's voice was harsh and difficult to understand, but we made out some of his one-sided conversation.

"I know who's cruddy well done this! It's those crudding animal rights nutters!"

All of us collapsed with smothered laughter.

"The cruddy garden's dug up, I tell you! There's holes all over the cruddy lawn! Those scumbags! I'd like to…and I can't get through the front door *or* the cruddy side gate! Somebody's blocked them up!"

Then the farmer turned round and walked back into his garden, still holding the thing to his ear and yelling at nobody.

Isabel sat up indignantly.

"C'mon out, you nasty person!" she ordered. "Come and get this lovely surprise we've spent so long preparing for you."

Robbo pushed her back down in the grass.

"Stay low!" he whispered. "He might a gone to get his killing stick."

But the farmer reappeared, with no killing stick in sight.

"I'm going to my farm now!" he shouted. "By the time I get

back, I expect to see at least one police car here! I can't even get to the cruddy garage without going through the back gate and round the outside of the garden! It's those animal rights nutters! They ought to be… AAAARGH!"

What he thought should happen to them was never made clear, for with a slurp and a squelch the chicken farmer stepped up to his chest in a pit of cow poo.

We forgot about being careful. We leapt in the air, we cheered and we rolled over and over, laughing until we ached. Mr P Stonehart's mouth fell open as he stared at us stupidly.

Suddenly there was a loud crack. Everyone dived low and froze. The noise had come from the house itself. The back wall had a black zigzag across it and one top window looked higher than the other.

"Hope the moles are all right," muttered Marian.

Slates from the roof, loosened by squirrels over the last week, started to drop off into the garden. The farmer was bellowing fit to burst. I'd never heard most of the words he was using.

"I think it's time we skedaddled back to the Hollow," said Hugo.

"Skedaddled?" said Mildred. "What kind of word is that?"

"One of Magnus's," grinned Hugo.

"And what are animal rights nutters?" asked Marian.

"Dunno," I said. "But if they're enemies of the farmer's, they must be all right. Listen! I'm going to creep over to the chicken farm. Revenge is sweet, but I want to check those birds are all right."

"No, Edgar!" said Marian. "You promised! We all said we'd lie low till it was over."

"Don't be stupid!" said Hugo. "The owls'll tell us what's happened. That's the arrangement."

"I can't help it – I feel responsible. I've got to know the chickens are okay."

We were ignoring the bellowing, but Robbo suddenly hissed, "Watch out!" and we saw that the farmer was trying to heave himself up out of the pit.

"Yo, good job one of us has got eyes," said Robbo. "Time to go!"

But it was hard to tear ourselves away.

Gloop, slurp, squelch went the muck as the farmer pushed with his forelegs against the solid ground around the pit.

There was another CRACK! and a fresh zigzag appeared on the house. Now the roof looked completely wonky and slates were sliding into the garden at an alarming rate. The farmer looked back with an expression of horror on his face, which had turned from red to almost white. He slithered back into the ooze with a groan and a sucking noise.

On top of the roof was a built-up smoke-hole. It suddenly keeled right over and looked as if it was going to slide off along with the slates. But it didn't. It just hung, suspended, at a peculiar angle.

The farmer gazed up at it, eyes popping, mouth wide open. Then he raised his forepaws in the air and roared, "I'll get you for this, you...you scumbags! Prison's too good! You'll die! I'm gonna kill you!"

Face contorted, he slurped about, trying to get out of the pit. This time it looked as if he might succeed.

"I think it really is time to go now," I said.

"I'm coming with you!" said Marian.

"No, you're not!" I said. "You'll make it more dangerous. It's easier for one animal to hide than two." I nuzzled her nose.

"I'll stay with my family for a few days and send a message with Aidan."

"Oh, be careful," whispered Marian.
"You too," I said, and we all melted away into the long grass.

CHAPTER THIRTY

The World Looks In

I was so cautious on my journey to the prison farm, sticking to hedgerows, lying low at the least little sound, that it was past midday when I arrived. Not that you could see the sun overhead. Every now and then it struggled to send a few rays through the cloud cover, but mostly the cloud won the fight.

As I crept over a ridge on the edge of Horn Wood, the farm came into view. My breath caught in my throat and I found my eyes filling with tears.

It had worked.

All the working out (mostly by Elfreda) and all the careful gnawing of squirrels, mice and voles had done the trick.

Of course, they couldn't tackle the whole farm. There were too many huge barns for a small group of animals to deal with. So they'd chosen the building right by the road. Then everyone driving by would be able to see what it was like inside.

The Horn Wooders had managed to get the walls to fall outwards while enough supporting beams remained to hold the roof up. For this wasn't a solid house built of baked clay. It was made of strange materials unknown to any animal. But they had worked out how to knock the outside down without harming the chickens.

The tattered remains of the walls, trampled and torn by badgers, foxes and deer, lay on the ground, while the birds had their first ever sight of the world outside. And the world outside could see in.

The chickens were still tightly packed in their cages, of course. Too dangerous to let them roam free, even if they were able. Many of them would be too sick. The last bit of the plan relied on the good will of humans.

I'd seen what I came to see, but somehow I couldn't leave it at that. Even though there were zoom-hounds (sitting quietly, not zooming) and even though a number of humans were walking round what was left of the building, I crept a little closer.

I wanted to see the chickens themselves. Flat on my belly, I wriggled until I was behind a fence in earshot of the humans. I could see through, but I hoped no one would notice me.

Two humans, a male and a female, were holding things up to their eyes and flashing lights at the cages.

"Wait till Mac sees these pictures," said the male.

"How can people treat animals like this?" said the female. "You wouldn't believe it unless you saw it for yourself."

A large male, almost entirely dark blue except for his face and forepaws, was asking a lot of questions and doing something with a tiny stick in one hand and a little white block in the other hand. Making squiggles, I supposed, and felt pleased with myself for knowing that.

But it wasn't really the humans that interested me. My joy at knowing the plan had worked turned once again to horror when I looked at the cages. I'd sometimes wondered if I'd exaggerated things in my mind, remembered it all as being worse than it really was. I hadn't.

And when I looked at the pitiful birds I knew that for some of them it was too late. We'd realised that. Not all the chickens could be saved. The kindest thing for some would be a quick death.

But that little white one peering about with interest. Not too late for her, surely? And the brown one squawking at the flashing lights – she seemed to have quite a bit of life left in her. If only someone would look after them properly, give them warm straw beds at night and let them peck around outside in the daytime.

Well, it was out of our paws now. We'd done what we could. I allowed myself to feel proud of thinking up the plan, though I was very aware how much had been done by other animals.

I jumped, as two of those others crept up on either side of me.

"Elfreda!" I whispered. "Ethel! Isn't it brilliant? Well done!"

"We're feeling pretty good about it," whispered Elfreda. "Now, the only question is – will it work? Are they actually going to be free, or will that nasty human build another prison for them?"

I laughed softly. "After what *we've* done, I hope he's not going to want to stay around."

"I want a full report when we're back at the earth," grinned Ethel.

"Thanks for helping, Ethel," said Edgar. "I know you thought we were making a bit of a fuss, considering they're 'only chickens'."

"Oh, no," said Ethel. "Even creatures as stupid as chickens don't deserve to be treated like that. Besides, the way I look at it, if they're not in cages, they'll be easier to get at."

"Oh, Ethel!" we groaned.

"Don't be such a hypocrite!" snorted Ethel to Elfreda. "I suppose you're going to give up roast chicken?"

"Well, no," said Elfreda, shamefacedly looking at me.

"Don't mind me," I said. "Everyone's got to decide for themselves. I don't mind other people eating animals that have had a nice life and a quick death, just so long as no one force-feeds them to me."

A zoom-hound growled to a stop and yet more humans arrived. Two more dark blue males got out of it, accompanied by...the farmer!

"You see?!" he yelled. "You see what those scumbags have done?!"

"Is that the Evil One?" whispered Elfreda.

I nodded.

"Hey, cool!" grinned Ethel. "He's got a purple face!"

"Not all the time," I said. "It's interesting. He seems to keep changing colour."

The farmer charged up to another male and female, not the ones with the flashing lights, and stuck his forepaw practically in their faces.

"You've got something to do with this, haven't you?" he shouted. "You and your cruddy organic farm!"

"Oh, it's *our* farmers!" I said. "I didn't recognise them."

"Now, now, sir!" said one of the dark blue males. "That's a very serious charge. You could get into trouble if you go round accusing people without any proof."

"Trouble!" roared the chicken farmer, jumping up and down. "Trouble!" He stopped jumping and put his face right next to the blue male's. "I'm having such a *nice* time! I wouldn't want to *spoil* it by getting into *trouble*!"

"Well, I think you *should* get into trouble," said one of the other farmers, the female one, "for keeping chickens in such appalling conditions."

At this, there was a chorus of clucking and "Here, here!" from the listening hens.

"I'd forgotten they could talk," said Elfreda, surprised.

Another zoom-hound screeched up full of yet more humans with flashing lights.

"I think we've done our bit," I said. "Everyone can see what it's like now. Let's go."

With a last look at the tumble-down building, the blinding lights, the bewildered chickens and the humans now milling everywhere, we turned and crawled away. Only when we reached the trees did we get up on all fours.

But trotting to Mum and Dad's earth I wondered, had it really worked? Would new walls be put up, or were the prisoners finally going to be free?

CHAPTER THIRTY-ONE

Every Creature Should Be Free

That night there were two celebrations, one in Horn Wood and one in the Hollow. I wondered if we should wait until we knew the final fate of the chickens, but I was outvoted. Everyone was so relieved and delighted that our plan had gone without a hitch that they felt they deserved a party.

The Hollow dell was full of animals dancing, passing round juice and mead, and nibbling on titbits that Edith seemed to have magicked out of nothing. ("I thought you'd succeed, my dears, and I've been making a few preparations.") Though I wondered where she'd found the ingredients, as nobody's cupboard was exactly full.

Robbo was finishing a rap specially written for the occasion and was greeted, as usual, by wild cheers from his fans. As the young rabbit rejoined the dancing, Harold held up his paw and asked for quiet.

"Well, I can't compete with that, Robert," he said.

"Yo, Stripy!" snorted Robbo indignantly.

He hated Harold calling him Robert.

"You do know I only do it to annoy, don't you, Robbo?" twinkled Harold.

"Hm, ain't no thing," muttered the disgruntled rabbit, as everyone laughed.

"As I was saying," continued Harold, "I couldn't possibly compete with our rapping rabbit, but I do have something to say."

There was more cheering – it seemed as though everything was going to get a cheer tonight – so Harold waited for it to die down, cleared his throat and began to speak.

"The Great Stag once told our friend Edgar that he was going against nature. He made a big fuss about following nature's way – in other words, if you're a fox or a badger you have to kill to eat. I think he has changed his mind since then, and it has been truly heartwarming to be joined in our great enterprise by other animals who do 'follow nature's way', but who still believe, like us, that every creature deserves a happy life."

Yet more cheers greeted this, and Harold once again had to hold up his paw and wait for them to calm down.

"In the light of this co-operation between animals with different ways of life," he went on, "I have myself written a few verses, although as I said before, I cannot compete with your, um, *rap*, Robbo. But perhaps you'd like to hear my little poem."

More deafening cheers and cries of, "Yes, come on Harold! Good old Harold!" until Robbo yelled, "Yo, be quiet folks and let the badger do his thing!"

Harold nodded at Robbo, cleared his throat a few more times and began his poem...

"Whether you follow nature's way,
Or think that killing's had its day,
One thing we can all agree,
Every creature should be free.
Free to skip and jump and run,
Feel the wind, enjoy the sun,
Sniff the air and root around,
Stretch their wings and peck the ground.
One thing we can all agree,
Every creature should be free,
No more cages, no more bars,
Free to see the moon and stars.
Dirt to roll in, dig a hole in,
Fields to gambol, trot or stroll in,
One thing we can all agree,
Every creature should be free.
So whether you hunt and kill to eat,
Or take a vow to touch no meat,
One thing we can all agree,
Every creature should be free."

By the time Harold reached the last "one thing we can all agree", every single animal joined in. And they didn't stop. I found both my forepaws being taken, as we all formed a line which snaked around the dell and then through the whole of Badgers' Hollow, all the time chanting, "One thing we can all agree, every creature should be free."

Harold stood, tapping his back paw and looking amazed, until Edith whispered, "Well done, my dear. I didn't know you were such a talented poet." Then she took both his forepaws and turned him round in a stately dance on the spot.

I managed to find Marian and we whirled breathlessly through the Hollow, laughing and chanting. But as we passed the entrance to one of the badgers' setts, I pulled us both free of the other dancers. Osbert was standing a little way inside. At first I thought he was alone, then I made out Emma, her paw comfortingly around her husband.

I hesitated, then, "Come on, you two, join the fun," I invited them.

Osbert smiled wistfully. "Not quite ready," was all he said.

I nodded understandingly, then me and Marian rejoined the dance.

CHAPTER THIRTY-TWO

The Spring Festival

A few weeks later, when Magnus and the other moles were back in the Hollow and everyone had stopped lying quite so low, a baby wood mouse skidded into Edith's kitchen. Marian and I were sitting with Edith, chatting after our evening meal. We stared at the mouse in astonishment.

It stood there shaking like a leaf in the wind and sobbing, "There's t-t-two…there's t-t-two great b-b-big…oh dear…"

"It's all right," said Marian, trying to stroke it with her forepaw, which was slightly bigger than the mouse.

"Here, have a drink," I said, offering it a bowl of water in which it would have drowned.

Harold, as usual these days, was dozing by the oven but the commotion woke him up. He looked carefully at the wood mouse and said, "How old are you, young feller-me-lad? You can't be more than a few days old."

"Now, Harold," said Edith. "Let's calm the poor thing down before we start asking for its life history."

But Harold's question had made the mouse stop shaking. It drew itself up to its full tiny height and said, "I'm three weeks old today...and I'm a *girl* mouse!"

We all laughed.

"Now what's the problem, dear?" said Edith kindly.

"There's two great big, enormous *owls* outside and they told me to tell you they want to see you. But my mum told me to stay away from owls. I thought I was going to get *eaten*!"

"Your mum's advice is very sensible in general," said Edith, "but those are the Hootingly-ffeatherclaw cousins, Aidan and Benedict. They won't hurt you, my dear – at least while you're round here. I'd stay away from them, though, if you ever venture outside Badgers' Hollow. In fact, I'd do what your mum says and stay away from all owls for the time being. Here, have a bit of hazelnut."

She fished a fragment of nut from her winter store and handed it to the baby animal, who started nibbling greedily. Harold shook his head.

"They shouldn't have started families yet."

"It's the mild weather," said Marian. "It feels like spring, so people want to start pairing off and having babies."

"Huh!" grunted Harold. "So much for Henry's big idea. Have one lot of babies and then stop. At this rate, we'll be completely overrun by midsummer."

"I never did think it was a very practical suggestion," sighed Edith. "It goes against nature."

"We've been talking," I said, "haven't we, Marian, and the only thing we could come up with was that animals would have to *choose* who could stay."

"Yes," said Marian. "One animal from each litter could live in the Hollow when they grew up, and the rest would have to make homes elsewhere. They could still visit, like us and our families."

"Now that's more sensible!" said Harold.

"I don't quite like it, but we've got to do something," said Edith, shaking her head. "We'll have to have another moot."

"Oh, come on!" I said. "I'm dying to know what the owls have got to say!"

The little mouse was clearly not dying to know the owls' message. She stayed in the sett, contentedly nibbling her hazelnut.

By the time we got outside, the Hollow dell was almost as full as it would be for a moot.

"Ah, halloooo, halloooo," hooted the owls together. "We've nyoooos for yoooo!"

"The farmer left without more adoooo," said Aidan. "He packed his bags and off he floooo."

There was cheering and stamping of paws on the ground. I had a picture in my mind of the farmer sprouting wings and taking to the air.

Benedict blinked severely round at everyone, until we were all silent again.

"The chickens are safe, with *your* farmers, that's whoooo," he said. "They've got some new barns and fields outside toooo."

The hurrahs and shouts that greeted these words almost deafened me. I could see Robbo and Isabel dancing a jig and Hugo and Mildred whooping and leaping about, but I just sat quietly and felt a warm glow spread through me. It started where I thought my heart must be and crept right to the white tip of my tail.

Marian sat with me, wearing her shining-eyed look.

"We did it," I said to her.

"*You* did it!" she answered.

*

As Marian had said, it was the season for pairing off and having babies. I was invited to lots of weddings, including those of Elfreda and Ethel. It was all great fun and seemed quite natural. But I couldn't help feeling a bit odd when I learned that Mum and Dad were expecting another litter. I was going to be a big brother!

To honour us for our role in the freeing of the chickens, Harold and Edith had suggested a triple wedding at the Spring Festival itself. Me and Marian, Hugo and Mildred and Robbo and Isabel were all going to be married as part of the celebrations.

"I hope you know what you're doin'," sniffed Robbo to me. "You ain't exactly known each other long!"

I remembered something Robbo had once said to me.

"Oh, us foxes don't hang about you know," I grinned.

"Just because she got a pretty face," said Robbo.

"Hiccupping hedgehogs!" I shouted. "What rubbish! She's much more than just a pretty face!"

"Huh, that's as maybe," said Robbo. "It's a serious business, y'know, gittin' married and raisin' a family."

"Hark at Grandfather Rabbit!" exploded Hugo, who'd been listening open-mouthed. "And how long did you know Isabel before you got engaged?"

"Yo, Fox-face, *we've* had a long engagement an'..."

The rest of the sentence was muffled as me and Hugo sat on him.

A bank of earth had been built in the centre of the dell and planted with spring bulbs and corms. Flowers seemed to be shooting up all over the Hollow, and now the dell was filled with blue and yellow, purple and white, as bluebells, crocuses and daffodils took over from the early snowdrops.

I wondered if every spring was this beautiful. I could hardly believe that I hadn't been born this time last year. So much had happened, and I wasn't even a year old.

With my help, Osbert had planted flowers on his family grave, where Cuthbert lay buried next to his parents.

"I brought him up, you know," said Osbert, "after Father and Mother died."

I nodded.

"He'd have loved all this," Osbert went on, "the Festival and the weddings. He always loved a party."

I didn't say anything, as Osbert wiped his eyes with the back of his paw.

But the next morning, as I was helping Edith in the sett, Osbert came bounding in.

"What's happened?" I asked. "You look like a different animal!"

"I had the most amazing dream last night," said Osbert. "At least, I think it was a dream. I was by the grave, in this dream, patting the earth down round the bulbs, when suddenly I looked up and there she was – the Spring Hare. I bowed down to her and she said, 'There's no need to bow down.' And then she said, 'Why are you so sad?'

'You know why, Lady,' I said.

'But you've planted flowers for the Festival,' she said. 'What does it mean, the Spring Festival?'

'It's about new life,' I said, 'about life returning after the winter.'

'Exactly,' she said to me. 'You know that winter isn't the end, and you know that death isn't the end.'

Then she said, 'What was the best thing about Cuthbert?'

'His cheerfulness,' I said, 'the way he loved life.'

'Well, do you think he'd have wanted you moping around?' she said. 'Grief has its place, but it's time now for the happy memories. You won't forget him, and you'll feel sad sometimes, but go and enjoy your life with your wife and children!'

And then I woke up. It doesn't sound that much when I try and tell you about it, but I feel quite different now."

Edith nodded.

"The year turns and we turn with it," she murmured.

I nuzzled Osbert.

"It was a very good thing," said Osbert quietly, "what you did with the chickens. I'm sorry I couldn't be part of it."

"That's all right!" I said. "We all understood... You know, Osbert, if you don't mind... I think I will move into Cuthbert's sett, after all. Marian really likes it – she thinks it's just right for a family – but I wasn't sure if it had too many memories for me."

"But they're *good* memories," beamed Osbert, "like the Hare said. Oh, I'm so glad. Somebody's got to live there, and I'd much rather it was a good friend of Cuthbert's. With space being a bit tight, it wouldn't have been fair to keep the rabbits out any longer... You can look after all that mead in the cellar, as well!"

I thought of Cuthbert sucking the honey off his paws, when he'd finished making the mead. At least two years, he'd said, before it'd be ready to drink. A long time in the life of an animal.

"Wonder what we'll be celebrating when we get round to drinking it," I said thoughtfully. "Whatever it is, we'll drink a toast to Cuthbert."

And now it was the night before the Festival and the triple wedding, and I couldn't sleep.

I tried lying curled up with my tail over my nose, and I tried lying stretched out, first on my left side and then on my right. I tried getting up and having a drink of water, and I tried lying still and thinking of nothing. Only I didn't seem to be able to think of nothing.

I was nervous.

Suppose I said the wrong thing in the ceremony, or the right thing at the wrong time? I'd been through it all with Harold and Edith, and it wasn't very complicated – but still…

And then I'd got to make some kind of speech! Well, I wasn't going to say much – Robbo would probably perform one of his raps and I couldn't compete with that.

There'd been so much to prepare, with everyone's families coming in the morning. Ethel had promised to be on her very best behaviour, but at this rate I'd be so tired I wouldn't know what I was doing.

Thank the Hare me and Marian weren't the only ones getting married! I didn't think I could have borne that. Even so, at the moment I felt I'd rather cross the death-strip without using the tunnel than go through this wedding ceremony.

I had to get some sleep!

Perhaps I needed a breath of fresh air.

I got up again and tiptoed up the tunnel to the entrance. And there, sitting outside in the cool night air, I thought I might have dropped off for a minute…

For in the dell, weaving her way among the flowers in a graceful dance of blessing, was the Spring Hare. Everything looked silver in the light of the spring moon, but the Hare most of all. She seemed to shed her own silvery light around her as she danced on her long hind legs.

I was entranced. I forgot how tired and nervous I was and just gazed at her, until I felt my eyelids drooping. A huge yawn engulfed me and I rubbed my eyes, but when I opened them again she was gone.

Had I been asleep, or had she really been there? I wasn't sure, but it didn't matter.

Suddenly my whole body thrilled with delight, just as it had when I first came to the Hollow and found other animals who thought like me.

Who cared about weddings, and whether I said anything wrong? I had Marian, and we had the whole of our grown-up lives in front of us.

I could see us, living in Cuthbert's old sett, happy just to be together. Then bringing up cubs and celebrating Yule and the other great festivals with all our friends in the Hollow.

"The year turns and we turn with it." That's what Edith always said.

There *was* meaning in life – I'd doubted it once, but now I knew. A deep meaning running through everything, even if you couldn't put it into words. Life was good!

I stood up on my hind legs and danced by myself in the moonlight.